# AMELIA'S KNIGHT

Amelia and her sister Ruth have mixed feelings when their impetuous mother decides they should stay with her sister, Sarah, in the harbour town of Whitby, for Amelia cannot envisage them finding suitable husbands there. However, once she has set eyes upon the gallant, but mysterious, Samuel Knight, Amelia's opinion changes ... But her father, Archibald, an intelligence officer in pursuit of villains and a chest of stolen government gold, views Samuel in a rather different light ...

VALERIE HOLMES

# AMELIA'S KNIGHT

*Complete and Unabridged*

**LINFORD**
*Leicester*

First published in Great Britain in 2006

First Linford Edition
published 2007

British Library CIP Data

Holmes, Valerie
    Amelia's knight.—Large print ed.—
Linford romance library
    1. Whitby (England)—Fiction
    2. Love stories
    3. Large type books
    I. Title
    823.9′2 [F]

ISBN 978–1–84617–605–0

Published by
F. A. Thorpe (Publishing)
Anstey, Leicestershire

Set by Words & Graphics Ltd.
Anstey, Leicestershire
Printed and bound in Great Britain by
T. J. International Ltd., Padstow, Cornwall

This book is printed on acid-free paper

# 1

Samuel awoke. His eyes were still tired, his vision blurred at first, but then they focused on a grey and gloomy mass of cloud. He swayed up and down in the bottom of the boat. He smelt the fresh salty air and shivered with the cold.

Sitting up quickly, he nearly blacked out. He hadn't felt so rough for a long time, but then it had been some party that Evangeline had thrown for him the night before at the inn near Calais.

She was quite a woman. He tried to smile at the image of the sultry Frenchwoman.

However, his dalliance had nearly caused him to be arrested as an English spy, caught on French soil, thanks to her jealous husband.

He chuckled as his senses began to clear. Perhaps he thought the time had come for him to settle down a little, or at least calm down his activities. The war had gathered strength and showed no sign of abating.

Although the trade was good, the channel was more dangerous to cross than it had been a year ago.

He took control of his coble as he steered back across what he realised was a troubled sea, and headed for home. Samuel was normally very careful, and kept a tight ship — or boat. He did not believe in leaving details to chance. This time, though, he had.

Was it the wine, the woman, or the blow to his head the Frenchman had landed him, hurling a stone that had found its target as he climbed into the vessel pushing it through the breaking waves? He had made it in a dazed state.

Once safely away from the shore, though, he had given in to the urge to sleep. Whichever was the cause, the result had been that he was now miles off course and headed into a violent storm.

For the next few hours he fought

against the elements. The coastline that eventually emerged before him was a rugged one of headlands and sweeping bays. It looked treacherous, as rocky scars reached out into the sea. He passed a small harbour and manoeuvred around a headland to a narrow harbour with red-painted houses clinging to the steep cliff banks.

He saw the unmistakable landmark and stared in disbelief.

'Whitby Abbey!' he exclaimed, as the realisation that he had been thrown miles of course. But he beamed as, once he had had his rest and filled his belly, he would be safe to go back to the Thames and to London. There, he would lose himself until he was a distant memory in the eyes of those who sought him.

He decided that as soon as he landed, he would make enquiries at the boatyards on the west bank about selling his boat.

It had become too well known. He would buy a ticket and travel to

London on a ship, with the 'respectable folk'. He smiled at his attempt at the local accent, as he entered the harbour.

The thought of a warm bath, good food and a new future filled his heart with joy. Samuel Knight was in control again, which was just how he liked it.

★ ★ ★

'Whitby! Why do we have to go to Whitby, Ruth? What's wrong with staying here?' The young woman threw her brush down on to the bed in a fit of fury. She had no reason to want to travel to a frozen north-easterly coastal town where they were more familiar with whales then their fellow man.

'Amelia, you judge people that you simply do not understand. Mother has family there and since Father will be away for nearly a year we are going to stay with them. They live in a grand house, Mother says their parties are the gayest in the whole area and that they own boats, land, sheep and property.'

4

Ruth was obviously impressed by all her mother had told her.

'Oh, I can't wait. We shall be able to go out on the seas with a bunch of sheep for company,' Amelia said and grabbed her hands to her chest. She was definitely not impressed.

'You are impossible, Amy, and you deserve matching to a Captain of a whaling ship, then you can be taken to the frozen extremities of the north sea, to show you how fortunate indeed you are.'

Ruth picked up the brush and placed it neatly back on the table by the looking glass. 'You had better dress, Amy. Mama will be so upset if you hold her up. She sees it as a chance for us to find good husbands. Here there are too many girls who come from more affluent families competing for the officers who return from France.'

'Aye, if they return.' Amy stared out of the window. 'There will be no more gentle green hills, my dear sister. Instead, we shall have twenty foot waves rapping at our windows, and gale force winds battering our doors, and the only men available will smell of fish, and . . . '

'Amelia! Ruth! Are you dressed?' The moment they heard the high-pitched shrill of their mother's voice the girls were a whirl of activity. 'Bessie, go up there and chase up those lazy daughters of mine or we shall be late and I will not tolerate it!' They heard the sound of the maid's running feet on the stairs. She ran into the room, and looked from one dishevelled girl to the other.

Ruth was trying to fix the last strands of her golden locks under her hat, and Amy still had her mass of ebony curls bouncing around her shoulders as she shrugged into her dress.

'Whatever will I do with you?' With all speed she had, she bossed, cajoled and helped the two young women into a respectable state. Within a few more minutes she had them paraded at the top of the stairs as respectable young maids ready to travel.

Their mother stood waiting impatiently at the bottom. She glared at them firmly, and then smiled, and instantly her face softened.

'My beautiful babies. Come, we must go. By the time your father returns to us we shall have found suitors for you both. Oh, then I shall spend years alone, getting ever older and more wretched, but that is the sacrifice a mother must make. With you by their sides any man would consider parading you in London.' She sighed at the thought.

'Then why go to Whitby, Mama?' Amelia asked, bewildered by her mother's reasoning.

'Because, my dear, we are going to pick the richest, prize cherries and educate them to move to London and mix with more affluent and respectable society. Clever plan, isn't it? The other mothers are competing with the city girls, old money. You should clutch the new and make it respectable. Oh, if only I had my time again.

'Mother!' Amelia said, most shocked, or so she appeared to be. 'Do you mean you would not choose Papa if you had your time over? Is he not respectable enough for you?' Amelia put her hand over her mouth in an exaggerated gesture of shock.

'Oh, no, no, you must never think such a thing, Amelia. I meant that you girls have so much more going for you that I ever had.' Her mother placed her arm reassuringly around Amelia and led her to the door. She was still quite flustered.

Amelia glanced back at Ruth over her mother's shoulder and winked at her sister, who shook her head at her.

Amy found the temptation to tease her mother irresistable as the older woman nearly always fell for Amelia's jibes and foils.

They all climbed into the carriage. Mother sat with her long-time maid, Bessie, at her side, both looking admiringly at the two sisters.

'Well, Bessie, what do you think we

shall catch in Whitby?' She clasped her hands together on her lap as the coach pulled off, their luggage stowed on top.

'A cold, Mama? Or perhaps a crab or two?' Amelia offered as possible suggestion.

'Silly girl, Amelia,' her mother responded. 'No, I mean you might meet a wealthy Captain of a fleet of ships, or the owner of the yards or even a member of the local landed gentry. Oh, the possibilities are vast, and your Aunt Sarah shall give you all the knowledge you'll need to shortlist them. Oh, what fun we shall have.' Her mother almost squealed with delight at the prospect.

'Perhaps so, as they are a little behind the fashion, I might find a knight in shining armour at a local joust and bag a Lord for my dear Ruth,' Amelia said dryly.

'That's the spirit, Amelia. We'll find someone suitable for you, and dear Ruth, shall have the pick of the bunch.

Oh, you are such good girls. Never a jealous word between you, perfection itself.'

*   *   *

Eventually an abbey appeared on the headland in the distance. Amelia craned her head to see as much as she could. 'Oh, Ruth, I can see the sea. It is quite spectacular, and an old abbey ruins. We're going to go down a steep bank, oh, what fun!'

Amelia saw her mother's cheeks pale as the brake on the carriage squeezed against the wheel, screeching, as they descended the steep bank into the small harbour town.

The coach pulled up outside an inn, which had the picture of an angel swinging above its door.

'We are here and safe, my girls. Now, stay calm. Do not be in a fluster. Everything will be well. We shall have something to eat and drink first, refresh ourselves and then we shall make enquiries as to how to get my sister's estates.'

The door was opened and Bessie was helped out. Amelia stepped down next and immediately crossed over to the harbour side, leaving Ruth to help her mother out of the coach. Amelia put a hand upon her hat and held it in place as gusts of wind blew in from the wild sea. She looked up to the east bank. The old church had pride of place on the steep slope, and the ancient abbey beyond.

Sea-gulls kwaarked and circled above them. Boats, ships and cargoes came and went. People whirled around, traders, barefoot children and respectable looking people alike. All seemed to be a hive of activity. She breathed in the fresh sea air and felt the energy of the place surge through her veins.

She looked down and saw a man taking a boat single-handedly towards the bridge. He looked over in her direction and smiled broadly at her. She laughed.

He was young, but older than her, obviously strong and sure of himself. He waved to her, and she boldly waved back.

'Amelia!' Bessie's voice boomed across at her from the other side of the road.

Amy looked back.

'Come here this minute!' the woman ordered. Her mother, Amelia could twist around her finger, and in truth she had little respect for her although she loved her dutifully, but it was Bessie who had always been her discipline, guardian and friend when she needed one to confide in.

'Coming,' she answered, but took a moment to glance back down at the man in the boat, but when she did the boat had gone. It had slipped under the bridge out of sight.

Amy made her way back to Bessie. Ruth and her mama were already seated at a comfortable table within the inn.

'You, girl, will be fit for no man, if you keep going on the way you are. You start acting more like your sister and learn some respect.' Bessie was waving a finger at her.

Amy looked humbly down at her, and said, 'I'm sorry, Bessie. Sometimes I get so excited I forget myself.'

'Don't try that out on me. It may work on your dear mother, but I was brought up in the real world and I'm not so easily taken in. So don't think you will lead me a merry dance, miss!' She stared straight into Amelia's eyes as they approached the inn.

'Bessie, you forget yourself!' Amy answered quickly, before swiftly opening the inn's door and joining her mama and Ruth. She could almost feel the supressed anger emanating from Bessie behind her.

Amy decided she would control her character for a few days until she understood this strange and fascinating place.

For the next half an hour she sipped a hot chocolate and ate her food with perfect decorum and contented herself with listening intently to their small talk.

Then he entered. Her mama and Ruth did not give his rather dishevelled figure a second glance, but Amy's eyes followed the tall figure as he walked over to the innkeeper and booked himself into the inn. He carried a small chest and a sailor's cloth bag, but there was something about his air that spoke of more than just a fisherman.

Whether he sensed he was being watched or not, Amy could not tell, but he saw her and winked discreetly in her direction. She grinned broadly, and then yelped, as Bessie kicked her under the table.

'Whatever is the matter?' asked her mama.

'Nothing, I stubbed my toe, that is all.' Amy glared at Bessie, who smiled sweetly back at her, then she looked back to the stranger, but once again he had gone, and Bessie's grin grew broader for a change.

# 2

Oh, that was splendid food, Bessie,'
Mama said, and looked at her empty
plate. 'Now, come on girls, eat up and
let's be on our way. No good dallying.
The sooner we surprise Aunt Sarah
with my two beauties, then the sooner
we can organise balls, soirees and
assemblies. It will be so grand.'

'To where, exactly, Mama?' Amy
asked, wishing they too could stay at
the inn, and then she might be able to
speak to her mystery man in the boat.

'We must find out where Consequence House is, in all haste. Perhaps it
is high up there towards the back of the
town, away from the hustle and bustle
of the place.' Mama nudged Bessie.
'Go and see if that driver of ours is
ready and if he has found out the way
to get there.'

Bessie shifted her rump off the chair

and made her way towards the outside doors.

'Consequence House?' Amy repeated, 'What is it a consequence of?'

'Don't take words too literally, Amelia. The name was most likely already given to it. Sarah was always such a bright and cheerful slip of a girl. I can imagine the frippery, drapes, chandeliers and gaiety within. Oh, I am so pleased we were able to rent out our own humble home for the season, as I'm sure once you have experienced such splendour you shall never wish to return.'

Amelia smiled at her sister. 'Consequence House,' she repeated. 'I like the sound of it. It opens up a whole myriad of possibilities as to how it came by its name.' She grinned impishly at Ruth who tried to listen intently to her mother as she rambled on with her image of what this estate would be like.

'You, Amelia, have your father's fanciful mind, always wandering, never satisfied with its surroundings, which is why of course he is off exploring Spain, whilst I am left to see that your futures are assured.' She sniffed indignantly at the weight of such a burden.

'My goodness, Mama. What a thing to say. Father should hear such a statement whilst he is working for the government and aiding the war effort by using his contacts. He is hardly on holiday. He could be in great . . . '

'Barcelona or anywhere for that matter, so it is best we do what we can here so that he need not worry anymore about us, and concentrate on his work.'

Ruth opened her eyes wide at Amy as if she had realised that what she was about to say was 'great danger'.

Sometimes the way Bessie and Ruth mollycoddled her mother made her feel quite sick. How would the woman ever cope with reality if it hit her hard in the face because the truth was always hidden from or softened for her?

She was about to complete her sentence, regardless of the conse- quences, when the door from the private rooms at the back of the inn opened and a well-dressed gentleman stepped out.

He had washed, changed and looked more relaxed but Amy recognised his tall muscular frame instantly.

He hesitated for a moment then approached their table.

'Good day, ladies.' He bowed low, and their mama was lost in admiration of his manner and dress.

'Good day, sir. We were just admiring your township,' their mother answered, obviously wanting to know if he were of the local gentry.

Close up, Amy could see his tanned face. He was obviously an outdoor man, not one for clubs and offices.

'I am afraid I am merely a visitor, but tell me, are you and your sisters staying at the inn?'

Amy had to look down as she caught his eye when he asked her mother the blatantly flattering question. Sisters indeed!

Her mother laughed sincerely and

childishly at his words. 'Sir, you are too kind. No, we are staying with my sister at Consequence House. We have yet to reach our destination but I can assure you, once settled, we shall have visitors to dine. I hope you do not have business of a pressing nature to take you away from the town just as we arrive.'

'I am undecided at present. I shall return to London soon, but may dally a little while.' He sneaked a quick glance at Amelia, but she did not return it. Their mother's eyes sparkled at the mention of London.

'Please, I am most remiss. You must excuse me for I am tired after our journey. This is my daughter, Ruth.' She waited for Ruth to smile and nod her head slightly at him, then she turned towards Amy, 'and this is my youngest daughter, Amelia.'

Amelia looked him straight in his deep blue eyes and smiled at him. 'Your pleasure,' she said, and looked away.

He took one of her hands in his and

kissed the back of it. 'Indeed, you speak only the truth.'

Amy blushed deeply, knowing he was playing her own sort of games out, in front of her mama, who glowed with pride that the handsome well-dressed stranger was showing a preference for her youngest daughter.

'You have the advantage, sir, as you have not introduced yourself to us, so I have no idea who has just molested my hand,' Any answered defiantly and her mother started to fluster because of Amelia's outspoken response.

'You are quite right, forgive me ladies.' He straightened up. 'I am Samuel Knight, of the Piccadilly Knights.' He bowed politely and, as Bessie returned to them, he made his excuses and left.

'Oh, girls, what did I tell you? We have already met one of the Knights of Piccadilly, what did I tell you?'

Amelia laughed, but controlled herself immediately as Bessie was trying to make sense of it all. As the group left the inn, Amelia's mother asked, 'Where are we going?'

'To Consequence House. We passed it on the way here. We have to go down a narrow cobbled street, beyond two old inns and then on towards the harbour. The steep house is on four different floors and overlooks the harbour. It had been both a refuge for desolate seamen and a school for the impoverished children and now belongs to your sister.' Bessie watched her mistress's face look crestfallen.

Amy could see the puzzled expression deepen as she tried to comprehend what was being said to her. 'But what about the grounds, her estates?'

'Did she say she actually owned the land, Mama? Or did you presume that from her letters?' Amelia asked with no hint of sarcasm or jollity.

'Well, I can't remember exactly, but she said she had never felt so rich in body and soul, but I have always been very astute and able to read in between the lines as well as the stated facts. She must use this as her town house. You wait and see! I bet she has an estate on the outside of town. You'll see.'

They all held tightly as the coach went along a cobbled street and they shook as the seat vibrated. Amy said nothing which was very rare. She and Ruth exchanged concerned looks, and Bessie stared down at her lap as she held their mama's hand.

Amy was too busy looking out of the window and realising the gravity of their mother's latest mistake. They had no house to return to, so no matter what was up ahead of them, they were stuck here for at least four months. Life was about to become very different and Amy thought, quite selfishly, very interesting indeed.

★　★　★

Samuel left the inn. This place was cooler than he was used to but, with a good quality greatcoat and hat, he could bear it, compared to the open sea in a storm.

He wandered for a while before seeing a sign for another inn. He stopped for a drink and decided to rent a chaise. If he was to stay one step ahead of his pursuers, then why not take that step sideways.

They would surely be searching the city, going to his usual haunts and contacts — Old Jeremiah near St Paul's, Molly in the Dials or Ping amidst the opium houses, not that he used or traded the stuff.

Even he had his own code, but Ping owed him his life, so he was a very useful contact to have. Who would think of seeking him hundreds of miles away from such valuable people in the London's underworld, to a small harbour town.

He smiled broadly and thought about the other attraction — Miss Amelia; a lady for certain, but one with a sparkle in her eye, a feisty temperament and a very pretty face.

The mother was a complete social climber, that was obvious, but the older sister was gentle and reminded him of his own dear mother, God rest her soul.

He would treat her with the greatest of respect, but enjoy a few socially acceptable meetings with her sister. He was sure the mother would encourage it and it would all serve to pass his time in a pleasant manner for a week or two before he returned and faced the music, or travel to the East.

There was a rough beauty to this coast. It was rugged and isolated, but attractive none-the-less. It was not long, however, before the beauty and image was spoiled as he rode towards the busy Alum works that were burning and transforming the landscape into the much sought after chemical, which was so desperately needed for dyeing so many items.

He turned back to the old harbour and watched from the headland as small boats came and went. How many of the fishermen had contraband stashed within their catch, he could not guess, but quite a high proportion, he supposed.

Samuel looked down at his hands as he held the chaise steady. For the first time in years he was almost overcome with emotion, for only three days ago they were tied behind his back, and the man holding a sword to his neck had threatened to kill him.

There would have been no wife, no child and no future. All that he had been would have been removed from this earth with no trace of him left. There would have been no epitaph even, on which people could have reflected.

He had never stopped to think about it before, but what was all this work for? He looked back over his adventures for the first time. Friends, made and lost, nothing stayed, no constants, so many near scrapes. It had always been a game to him — a challenge.

He had taken the risks, made his profit and when he came out richer and ahead of the other players he hungered for the next venture, but not in the last few months.

The net had tightened almost around his own neck. Samuel stared at his hands and they shook. It was time to thank his lucky stars that he was fit and healthy.

Samuel thought again about the face of the young lady, Miss Amelia, so fresh, full of life and ready to be released from her mother's skirts. His hands stopped shaking and he smiled. It was time Samuel Knight became respectable.

He had built up his wealth and now needed to build himself a nest. Not an empty one though, for now he needed a partner who was young, healthy, vibrant and willing. He flicked the reins of the horse and steered the chaise back towards Whitby.

It was time to settle down. He would start anew, and where better to start than a house called Consequence, for wasn't everything in life just that?

★ ★ ★

It was with a much lighter heart that he returned the chaise and entered the inn. He enquired as to the ladies who had been in earlier. However, they had left.

He decided to return to his room, order some good food and wine and draw up a plan. He had to have a family, a believable or plausible past and a convincing present. Then tomorrow he would study his prey so that their paths accidentally crossed once more. Samuel was feeling a very happy, confident and optimistic man.

★  ★  ★

The coach pulled up in front of the tall, narrow, whitewashed house. Their baggage was unloaded and Bessie lifted the large brass lion door knocker, letting it fall to announce their arrival. The carriage moved off. It would be stabled at a nearby inn.

After a few moments a lady opened the door. She was quite tall and slim.

Amelia recognised a striking resemblance between her and Ruth straightaway.

The woman's greying hair was fastened upon her head neatly in a bun, under an elaborately worked lace bonnet. Her dress was quite plain, and an apron was wrapped around her thin body to protect the quality fabric. This was not the image of affluence Amy had been expecting for her mother's description of her sister and her opulent lifestyle.

'We're looking for the mistress of the house,' Bessie said, whilst the three of them stood in surprised silence. 'Our arrival is expected,' she added as the lady merely looked at her, perplexed.

Amelia realised she had made a bad misjudgement. This lady was most definitely her Aunt Sarah, and this narrow house, rather like its mistress, was her *estate*.

'Aunt Sarah. It is I, Amelia.' She spoke over their maid's shoulder and discreetly moved Bessie back so that it was Amy who was standing beside her mother.

The woman looked a little confused by Bessie's rather abrupt approach, but she smiled at Amelia obviously delighted to see them all. Instantly it placed some colour into her pale complexion.

'Amelia, you are all grown up, and Ruth, what a beauty you are!' She then turned to her sister, Prudence, who was so shocked by the turn of events that she could not form any words to greet her sister.

Bessie stepped back and saw to the baggage. She was blushing profusely and trying not to look at the lady she had unintentionally insulted.

The three women were led into the narrow hall of their new home. When Bessie entered she looked nervously at Sarah. 'I'm so very sorry, ma'am. What must you think of me?'

Sarah patted her shoulder and smiled warmly at her. 'I think you are a very loyal servant who I have heard only good reports about for many years. One simple mistake will not take that away from you, now will it?'

They were all shown into a homely little parlour at the front of the house. There were just enough seats for them all to be seated comfortably. The small room was filled with samplers, embroidered furnishings, cushions and trinkets. It was a mass of textures and colours.

Amelia loved it. Far from an aloof woman that she had expected, with an enormous house and an estate too vast to walk around, this was a real home, and so obviously loved.

'Prudence, please take off your coat, and sit by the fire in my comfy chair. I'll ask Helen to fetch us a tray of tea and scones, and freshly-made Yorkshire parkin. That will be splendid. Then you can tell me all about what has been happening to you. It must be horrid, whatever it is, Prudence, but you must disclose all. Having to rent out your home like that and stay here. Never you mind, though, you'll always be welcome so long as I have a home to share.'

She turned to face Amelia. 'Whatever has happened must have been tragic. I have never seen her at such a loss for words.' She held Prudence's hand as if to comfort her. 'You shall share my room. It will be just like when we were girls again. We can have nice cosy chats.

'The girls will sleep on the floor above us and Bessie can share with Helen in the loft room. All will be so cosy and well.' She slipped silently out of the room.

'Share,' Prudence repeated.

Bessie giggled. 'The attic room! I hope you won't need me in a hurry as I'm not as nimble as I used to be.'

Ruth smiled nervously at her, but Amelia watched her mother and said nothing. Her heart felt for the bewildered woman. If people hadn't played along with her flights of fancy, this situation would never have come about. Whatever would her father say when he found out what she had done. She dreaded to think.

Amelia stared out of the window and looked beyond the houses to some steep steps that went up to the church atop the headland and the abbey beyond. As soon as she could escape she would run up there and explore this most intriguing and unusual place.

★   ★   ★

Samuel returned the chaise and then walked over the swing bridge to the old part of town. People looked at him as he passed, noting the stranger, but carried on with their business. He asked directions and soon ascertained where the carriage had dropped the ladies off.

All the time the air was filled with busy sounds, the birds, waves hitting rocks and breaking, the boat-builders, house-builders, children and women talking and shouting. This was a raw place, but one filled with energy and life. As he turned around and saw the steep church steps his attention was taken by the tall house across the street, Consequence House!

So this was the sister's estate. He chuckled to himself. Never mind, the mother may be delusional, but the daughter was worth pursuing. He immediately entered the inn and enquired if they had a room available that overlooked the church and abbey. They did, because most visitors preferred to have a view of the harbour.

He also saw a cottage farther along the street which was for sale. He pondered. If the lady was staying the season, he may consider it. For now, he would content himself with being neighbourly and watching for a chance to coincidentally meet Miss Amelia again.

He wasted no time and returned to fetch his baggage. He had paid for the night, but could well afford to leave the landlord the money. The sooner he took up residence in his new rooms the better. The morning would be Sunday and what better way to meet respectably, but in church.

# 3

What do you mean, sergeant? How could he get away from you? I had a man positioned near that inn. He told Jerome the minute Knight was drunk. All they had to do was tip off the French and arrest him. Then he'd have rotted in some French jail, if he wasn't kicked to death first. Knight would have been forever out of our hair. What went wrong?' The man in the red jacket, with stripes on his arm slammed his fist firmly down on to the table.

'Lieutenant Morris, I know it should have been straightforward, but he's a tricky character. He has had a lifetime of slipping away. But Jerome was certain he hit him as he climbed into his boat — the Marie-Anne. No-one has seen him since. The last lot of brandy arrived with no interference from him. He could have lost his nerve, sir.'

'Knight! You must be joking! He doesn't have any nerves to lose. He's a speculator and adventurer.' The lieutenant shifted uneasily. He did not believe he was finally free of Knight's interfering shadow on his affairs. Not until a body had been found.

'None of his women and none of his contacts have been seen with him or have admitted to seeing him since we returned. No-one appears to know where he is. His boat could have gone down, sir. There was a bad storm that night and it is a treacherous sea.' The sergeant was trying his hardest to appease Morris's doubt. However, it was not working.

'You better hope so, Dougie, because if he gets in the way of one more of our runs, I'll have him, and any useless son of a sow who lets him slip through his fingers. Do I make myself clear, sergeant?' The man was openly livid.

'Yes, sir. It won't happen again, sir. I'll see to it myself.' The sergeant saluted his officer.

The sergeant left the barracks cursing Knight. Too many times he had shadowed their operation then whisked a catch away from them to take the profit himself. He was a slippery character, but he would not get Douglas McBride into trouble again.

As soon as he found out where Knight was hiding, he'd eliminate him, removing the problem once and for all. He knew too much, anyhow, about how the lieutenant and he lined their pockets. No, this time Samuel had stepped beyond the pale.

⋆  ⋆  ⋆

Amelia looked out over the roof tops that were below her own bedchamber window. This mish-mash of houses seemed to almost nestle together. Very narrow alleyways existed between the buildings and small yards. It would take quite a while to learn all the pathways around this place but the prospect of doing it appealed to the child still within her. Far from seeking a suitor, she was more interested in having fun and adventure.

Surely this was the ideal place to start. She was falling in love with this rambling, cold place.

She stared at the boatyards on the west bank and the new arc of houses being built on the yonder cliff. Then she watched the activity of the harbour. She had never had so much activity visible from one window before.

At home she had seen deer, a lake and a copse of trees. Static beauty. It did not compare favourably to the activity, noise and colour that greeted her senses here.

There were the smells, from the salty air, fish, the bakery down the street, and yet more than she could presently discern. The place had a history waiting for her to investigate upon the cliff, the old Abbey where St Hilda once walked and prayed, and the unique church below.

Their bedroom was narrow, like the

house itself, and had two small beds within it, and a small trunk under the little window between them. The handmade quilts were lovingly worked.

Ruth stared around her in disbelief. 'How do we dress in here?' she asked. 'Please tell me we came to the wrong room and this is the maid's quarters.'

Amelia laughed. 'It is ours. It is 'cosy' as Aunt Sarah says. We shall be warm here, no high ceilings or large changing rooms . . . '

'You are mad, if you think this is going to be fun, Amelia. It is nothing short of dreadful,' she said. 'How do we dress in here?'

'Carefully and in turns,' Amy answered, 'and it will be fun, we shall make it fun because Mama is downcast enough. We shall find an assembly room and try to appease her, even though this whole mess is her own misguided fault.'

'What will Father think when he receives her letter. She sent one to the Horse-Guards to forward to him, wherever he is.' Ruth sat down on the bed which was surprisingly soft.

'He will know we are staying with a dear lady. He will also know that his wife is capable of making very bad decisions and he will come to save us from our predicament once he is free to.' Amy looked back out of the window as Ruth left to rejoin their mama, unconvinced by Amy's words.

Her attention was caught by the figure crossing the swing bridge, carrying his bag and trunk. It was the stranger, Samuel Knight.

She watched him make his way down the cobbled street, she lost his progress for a while but, just as she was about to rejoin Ruth, he appeared once more, walking into the inn opposite. 'Whatever is he playing at?' she spoke her thoughts aloud.

'Whatever is who playing at, Amy?' Ruth asked. She had returned wondering what kept Amy from coming.

'Oh, nothing, just a young boy up to a prank, no doubt.' She smiled at Ruth. 'Come, we must return to the parlour and enjoy our 'parkin',' she answered brightly.

Ruth and Amelia entered the parlour to find their aunt and mama sitting by the fire already taking their tea and cake.

'Girls, I wondered where you had got to,' Aunt Sarah said.

Their mama was staring into the fire, sipping tea from a china cup and staring aimlessly into the flames.

'We were admiring the view from our room,' Amelia said, and Ruth glanced at her a little uncertainly. 'Can we go for a walk later?' Amy asked, her heart really meaning now.

'Well, if not later, tomorrow, after church. St Mary's is a beautiful church with enclosed pews, quite unique. If your mama feels up to it, that is.' Her aunt looked at Prudence, most concerned, and placed a hand upon the woman's knee. 'Are you all right, dear?'

Prudence placed the cup down upon the side table. 'No, not really. I am most perplexed. There is so much I do not understand, Sarah.' Her voice sounded irritable.

'Then let us speak about it and perhaps between us we can sort your problem out satisfactorily. Is it Archibald, Prudence? Has he gone missing or something uncertain?' Sarah asked tenderly.

'No, certainly not! He is still gallivanting in Spain and I am left to find suitors for my two dear daughters, and as you can see, they are not getting any younger you know. Soon they will be considered old maids and left at home with me, whilst Sally Pinkerton's girls marry the best of young men around. The situation is intolerable.' Prudence clasped her hands together, placing them on her lap.

Sarah looked at Amelia who was stifling a grin. 'Who is this Sally Pinkerton?' she asked.

'She lives in the next estate. Her husband is a banker and she has three, rather plain and talentless daughters, two of which have married and they are our age, Aunt. This worries Mama,' Amelia answered with a straight face, but her cheeks were flushed and her eyes sparkled.

Sarah stared at her sister. Her expression was one of complete confusion. 'If you are so set upon matching these two lovely 'young' girls, to beaus, and Archibald is fine, why have you come to stay in Whitby for the season?'

'Because of your letters, Sarah,' Prudence answered, as if that statement explained all.

'Whatever do you mean?' Amelia noted a slight look of amusement in Sarah's expression as if she was beginning to realise that Prudence had not understood what she had written at all.

'You told me that your husband had left you adequate finances for your lifestyle,' Prudence said and nodded to stress her point.

'Yes, my dear, Donald did.' She looked around her at the room. This lovely house means everything to me and it is paid for and belongs to me. What else could I ask for but the home I desire?'

'But you always had such tastes for elegant and fine things and talked of the day when you would live in a castle or a grand hall . . . I presumed that day had come.'

'Oh, Prudence, that was silly talk from an immature woman, that's all. I passed that stage years ago. No, I learned what was important in life many years since. I am perfectly happy here. It is both cosy and comfortable.' Sarah smiled at Ruth and Amy, who beamed lovingly back at her.

'You said that you were the richest woman in Whitby and were fortunate to have some truly great friends. Tell me you did not write that? Can you deny it?' Prudence was most defiant.

'Prudence dear, I was not speaking literally about my wealth. I was saying how blessed I felt that I had been given such good — no, you are right, great friends, I feel, in a spiritual sense, the richest of all people in the town. Not in an earthly monetary sense of the word, but in the sense that I lack for nothing and consider myself so fortunate to have my health and be so happy here.' Sarah was staring at Prudence, obviously now understanding that her sister had not changed over the years. She still believed the girlish immature dreams of their youth.

'But what of your estate? You said it was vast with open land behind your home and views from your bedroom that spanned to the distant horizon. True you never mentioned your deer, but you did say it was vast.' Prudence was standing almost accusing Sarah, with her own words.

'Oh, my dear Prudence, you are so very fanciful, and at your age! If I'd known you would put this inference on my words I would have chosen different ones.

'The open land to the back is the vast moors. It does not belong to me alone, or at all, and from the front my bedchamber overlooks the harbour and the expanse of the open sea to the distant horizon, not a personal estate.'

Prudence shook her head. 'If only we had known what you truly meant, I should never have rented out our dear home, or if I had, I should have planned to take them to York or Harrogate and introduce the girls to society there, but now I have neither the time to arrange dresses or the funds available to pay for appropriate rooms to stay there.

'Oh, what a mess. If only I had realised what your words meant, that they were merely a smokescreen to divert my understandable concern for you. You could have come with us and we may have even found you a retired colonel or some-such who would have been glad of your companionship,' Prudence sobbed.

Sarah put her hands on her hips. 'Well, Prudence, you read into my words what you wanted them to say. You asked to stay with no explanation as to your real motives and you are now stuck with that choice. Your girls are beautiful and intelligent so let them have some healthy air in their lungs, enjoy their exercise and find humour in their last season without a man to pin them down. They will not age so quickly as you and I will now . . . '

Prudence gasped and Amy struggled not to clap her hands with glee that at last someone knew how to speak to, and handle, her mama.

'Don't meddle in my life. You are a woman of the world, but regarding myself I have no wish to keep any old man company unless he amuses me. So please do not concern yourself there, for I am more than able to fend for myself. Now finish your tea and we shall change and go for a walk. I think we all need some fresh air.' She looked at Ruth and Amelia. 'Girls put some warm clothes on, I shall see to your mama.'

# 4

Within half an hour, Prudence had taken to her small bed, feigning exhaustion because of the length of the journey and the shock at the change of circumstance of her sister. She was fatigued and ordered Bessie to make her some chicken soup to build her up. Ruth offered to sit with her mama, and fussed over her, but Amelia was disgusted with the pair of them. Sarah still put on her coat, hat and gloves and headed for the door.

'Aunt Sarah, may I come out with you, please?' Amy asked as her aunt reached out for the handle of the door.

Sarah stopped and looked at Amy, then smiled warmly at her. 'Of course you may. I should be glad of the company. Do you wish to ask your mama's permission first?' Sarah looked at her and raised an eyebrow.

'No!' Amy said, as she placed her hat upon her head. 'I don't, I just want to be allowed to go out and explore the town.'

★  ★  ★

They were outside and up the slope towards the steep church steps within minutes.

'I'm sorry that Mama has burdened you with us for all the wrong reasons, Aunt Sarah.' Amy linked arms with the woman next to her as a natural reaction.

She felt her aunt squeeze her arm to her side in a gesture of acceptance, which also appeared automatic and a natural response.

'Don't apologise for my sister's foolhardiness. She has not changed in all these years, but I love her very much all the same. Mind you could do worse for yourself than some of these local men. They work hard.'

Amy's smile dropped, and Sarah laughed.

'Don't worry. I shall not engage in matchmaking. I shall let your dear mama humour herself with that. She hasn't changed over the years other than in her weight which is twice what it once was.'

'You are very fond of her, though, aren't you?' Amy asked and saw Sarah smile.

'Yes, she has always been a dear day-dreamer. I thought life might have mellowed her, but instead it has humoured her. But you, girl, are very different. Where shall we go first?'

'Over there, by the edge. Let us look out on the sea. It is so beautiful, yet treacherous.'

After they had stayed as long as they could bear to against the cold wind, they returned down the path towards the church.

Amy looked up and smiled as, there in front of them, was the handsome figure of the stranger, Samuel Knight.

Sarah side-glanced at her. 'Do you know this man, Amy?' she asked quietly.

'We are acquainted. His name is Samuel Knight, and we met at the inn earlier. He introduced himself to Mama, Ruth and I. He comes from London's Piccadilly area.'

'Does he, dear? Then he must be quite lost,' Sarah said sarcastically, and Amy stifled a laugh.

Amy shared what little detail she knew about him but omitted to mention she had seen him move into the inn across the street. He was her mysterious stranger and she wanted to unravel his mystery herself.

'Hello there. How opportune that we should meet again so soon.' Samuel removed his hat as they approached revealing his neatly-cut dark hair. It was fashionable and he was very confident.

'Mr Knight, what a surprise. Have you decided to stay and explore the area?' Amelia asked in her most pleasant manner.

'Yes, Miss Amelia. You must forgive me, but I'm afraid I only know your first name.' He looked from Amelia to Sarah.

'This is my niece, Miss Branham, Mr Knight. I am Mrs Henshaw. I live in Whitby and, as you may be aware, Miss Amelia will be staying with me.'

Amelia saw the confidence with which Sarah addressed him. She was obviously used to dealing with people of all classes and her posture was firmly held.

He seemed to sense her wariness of him and he adjusted his focus to Sarah instead of looking so much at her.

'I am delighted to meet you. It is a beautiful, yet lonely place. I am a stranger here, staying at the inn down there, and so I know no-one and am not familiar with the town, yet. However, it is very attractive and has a sense of purpose about it that I feel drawn to explore.' He looked around at the church. 'Most striking,' he remarked.

'I am sure you will find it to your liking. After all, sir, you manoeuvred your way into the harbour without any bother,' Sarah said dryly, and Amy could not help but suppress a grin.

'Yes, however, I have decided that the sea is not a place for me and promptly sold the boat. It was one toy I can live without. In fact, I steered so far off course, my whim could have cost me my life. I came back a changed man, Miss Branham . . . ' he turned to Amy, 'from now on my feet shall stay on terra-firma.' He smiled politely at both of them.

'So you shall be taking a coach back to London then, and not a ship?' Amelia asked.

'Eventually, I may, but not yet awhile. Ladies, I am being inconsiderate making you both stand out here in the cold. Would you care to enter the church or perhaps I could treat you both to a traditional meal at the inn's restaurant. I understand it is well thought of locally.'

Amelia glanced at Sarah. 'Perhaps, if you are attending the church service tomorrow, sir, our whole party may take lunch at the Phoenix when Amelia's dear mama will be with us also.' Sarah stared straight at him and Samuel met her gaze with a pleasant smile.

'What a splendid idea. I shall look forward to being a part of a family group.' He stepped back and fingered his hat with his gloved hand.

'Good, that is settled then. Tomorrow you can tell us all about your own family, Mr Knight.' Sarah linked arms with Amy again. 'Come, we must return to your mama before she worries herself as to where you are. Good day, sir.'

'Good day, Mrs Henshaw, and I shall look forward to tomorrow's service, and gathering, Miss Branham.' He replaced his hat. The wind blew the cape of his greatcoat so it flicked over his broad shoulders.

★ ★ ★

The ladies started the descent down the steep steps as Samuel turned to walk towards the church. It was when Amelia screamed that he came running.

She had glanced back to take one last look at him and not focussed on where she was putting her feet. Her footwear was not designed for walking on wet stones and she slipped. She landed with an undignified thump on her rear.

'Amelia, are you alright, my dear?' Sarah bent low to her. Immediately Samuel was there.

'Does your ankle hurt, Miss A . . . Branham?' He, too, crouched down by her. He looked at her shoes. 'I think you shall have to invest in some sturdy boots if you intend to go for walks around here.'

Sarah looked at her. 'Can you stand on it?' she asked, as rain started to pour down from the sky.

'No need.' Without waiting for her to answer her aunt, he scooped her up in his strong arms. 'If you would lead the way, ma'am, I shall bring her down before the storm breaks and we all take a soaking.'

Sarah led the way quite happily. Amy placed both her arms around his neck and, as he carefully made his way down the many steps, their eyes met and they both smiled broadly, enjoying the intimacy of the moment.

Her ankle was fine, his arms were muscular and they both liked being so close. However, as they neared the bottom of the steps, she released her hold on his neck and placed her hands in her lap, looking discreetly down at them, as Sarah turned to see the concerned look of Samuel as he stopped to catch his breath at the bottom.

'Where to now, ma'am?' he asked as if he had no idea where her aunt's house was. Amy glanced at him accusingly but he ignored her.

'My house is just here.' She pointed to it then opened the door. Sarah stepped back and let him carry Amelia inside to the parlour. Carefully he placed her in the chair by the fire. Outside the rain came down in torrents driven by the wind.

'I really think it will be fine. I merely slipped, but thank you for being so gallant.' Amy blushed slightly as both Samuel and Sarah fussed over her.

'You were very kind. I insist you stay at least to join us for a warm drink, until the rain abates.' Sarah pointed to a chair by the window. 'Please make yourself comfortable, Mr Knight.'

'I only have to go twenty paces to the inn, but if I am not intruding, a warm drink would be very welcome.' He removed his hat once more.

'Give me your hat and coat, man, and I shall organise a tray. I won't be more than a minute or two.' She looked pointedly at Amy before she left.

'Miss, I hope you don't think me forward . . . ' he began.

'Sir, you are very . . . forward, but I am flattered by your attention and your strong arms.' She smiled warmly at him.

'I should love to talk to you, walk with you again, if the opportunity should present itself, but of course not so as to blemish your reputation.' He looked ill at ease, as if, in speaking so boldly he may have overstepped the mark.

'Perhaps opportunities may present themselves, should my sister and I take a promenade, for instance, once we are more familiar with the place and I have some suitable attire. Perhaps we could walk together.'

'That would be splendid!' he said, as the door opened and Sarah returned.

'What would be splendid?' she asked innocently.

'To attend the assembly rooms on the west bank on Saturday. I understand they have functions each Saturday and the local 'nobility' attend.' He looked at Sarah. 'Would you recommend them?'

'I'm afraid I could not as I have never been.'

★   ★   ★

For the next month, the meetings between the sisters and Mr Knight were quite frequent. Even Prudence and her aunt seemed to approve of Mr Knight's occasional presence on their outings, although Amy saw her aunt often deep in thought as if weighing up any detail he let slip of his past, but they were very few.

Ruth had taken to sketching in the church, which was very convenient for both of them, because Mr Knight would often stray in, as he went on his daily walk up on the cliff, so whilst Ruth chatted animatedly with James, a fellow spirit interested more in art than his father's shipyard, they would wander up to the upper gallery and sit at a respectable distance on one of the pews.

They had met James as he was just starting on an oil painting of the church's interior. It was he who had inspired Ruth to try drawing inside instead of wrapping herself against the cold wind and perching on a stool outside, overlooking the harbour.

★   ★   ★

'Miss Amelia . . . Amy, has your mama decided to stay here?' Samuel asked her, listening attentively for her answer.

'She has no choice. Our home is rented out for the next two months, then I have no doubt she will pack up and move us quickly back there. I suppose she will feel sorry for her sister, feel magnanimous that she has spent some months with her, and then rapidly plan her next folly to find suitors for the pair of us.' Amy blushed wondering if she had spoken out of turn.

'Somehow, I don't think your sister will be so keen to leave here.' He nodded to the pew below them.

Amy peered down and for the first time saw what had been happening whilst her sights had been fixed on Samuel. James was holding Ruth's hand in his, discreetly and tenderly, as they sat together.

Amy leaned back grinning to herself. Oh, Mama! Perhaps she did the right thing after all.

'So that is why Ruth has ceased to

complain about the bitter weather here.'
Amy shook her head, amazed at her
own lack of alertness.

'You really had no idea?' Samuel
asked her, quite amazed.

'No, I must be slipping . . . or
preoccupied.' She blushed slightly.

'Amy, do you like me enough to
consider my asking your mama for your
hand in marriage?' He slid along the
seat until he, too, was holding her hand
tenderly.

He was half perched on the pew
whilst one leg was supporting his
weight on the floor, as if he were half
kneeling. His colour was high and he
seemed ill at ease.

'Oh, Samuel, you are proposing to
me?' Amy asked, as if a little shocked by
his boldness.

'Yes, I am. Does the idea appeal to
you?' He stroked her hand as if coaxing
a positive response from her.

'Yes, but Samuel, you are so mysterious. I know so little of you, even less of
your family and what you really do in

life. I mean, where would we live? Here or in Piccadilly? Would your own parents accept the likes of me for a daughter-in-law? Do you really love me?' The last question was said softly.

'Yes, that is the one question I can answer honestly and with no doubt. I love you with all my heart and want to be with you, wherever we choose to live. I have enough wealth to do whatever you wish me to. For you, Amelia, I would change everything, but you have to accept me as I am, and not ask questions about my family or pedigree, because they simply do not exist.

'I was an orphan. Born in the slums of London, raised by the city's charity, covering basic needs and little love, but I am no longer poor. I have made my own life, gained a decent education, thanks to reading many books and with the help of a learned friend who taught me to read, and I have travelled far.

'My past is one of an adventurer. However, my future I want to be shared with you. Can you find it in your heart to trust me, love me, and help me to have the family I never had and treasure it above all else?'

Amy lifted his hand to her cheek. 'Only if you let me share the odd adventure with you before I become heavy with child and tied to this perfect home that you seek.' She squeezed his hand affectionately, 'but you must remember nothing is ever perfect. That is an impossible dream to achieve.'

He hugged her like he would never let her go, and she felt so relaxed in his arms. 'I knew you were the one for me, and I you, the minute I saw you on the quayside, but I don't know how your father will view our match. He is in the army, I gather?' He sat back, smiling happily at her.

'Yes, that is correct; he works for the Intelligence Service, undercover and behind the enemy lines. He, too, is an adventurer, and enjoys taking great risks. We never know where he is.' Amy watched the smile fade from his face.

'What is wrong with that, Samuel?'

'Nothing, it is just that he may be the one person who can help me out of a difficult situation I find myself in. He could be the person who could help me with an important issue of the disclosure of dishonesty amidst the army's officer ranks, but only if you would help me to get a message to him. Could you? I ask a lot, and it may be involving you in some danger.'

'We have our mail sent to him via his offices in London. I could send a letter to him if you could explain yourself more clearly,' Amy offered, wondering quite what she was getting herself involved in.

'Could you ask your sister for a sheet of her drawing paper and I shall write down the names of two officers who are seeking me as we speak. I know the details of their illegal trade. They use the war to feather their own nests.

'I have foiled them on three occasions, where contraband should have found its way back to England, but I understand that if I return to London and they hear of it, I shall be 'removed' permanently,' Samuel explained and Amy looked at him horrified.

'Samuel, we shall write today. You must be made safe. But tell me, what were you doing to know of their illegal dealings and how did you foil them? What became of this contraband?' she asked and saw his cheeks flush slightly as his eyes looked around God's house as if searching for appropriate words to explain.

'That answer is one I can only discuss in complete confidence to someone I can trust implicitly.' He stared at her, and appeared at a loss as to what to say next.

'Then think about the words you can use to divulge your secrets and when I return you will trust me with the truth, for I will only marry an honest man. That honesty had to start between the two of us or we have no future together.'

She ran down the stairs to Ruth

straightaway, excited as her wish was being granted. She was uncovering her mystery man's secrets and saving him — from himself and his pursuers in the process.

# 5

Whatever is the meaning of this interruption, sergeant? Haven't I told you before I am never to be disturbed when I am with — company?

The sergeant looked at the 'lady' in question who he recognised instantly as the wife of a fellow officer. Her husband was conveniently away on a tour of duty.

'I apologise. However, sir, I would not presume to interrupt your discussions if the information I had was not of the most urgent nature.'

'Please excuse me, Margarita, I shall only be a moment.' The lieutenant ushered the sergeant from his room. 'This better be good, Douglas, or you shall be doing night duty for the next two weeks!'

'His boat has been spotted mooring, and we thought we had him at last. My man waited until the craft was securely anchored, then pounced, but . . . '

'Knight? You have him at last! Where?'

'Yes, Knight. We thought we had him, but damnation! It was just an honest fisherman landing his catch to take to market. He — Knight — wasn't in it.

'The man had bought the boat from him recently.' The sergeant smiled at the lieutenant.

'Where, man, where is he?' the officer asked anxiously, desperate to know.

'He bought it from a man who fits his description, in Whitby.' The sergeant saw the pleasure instantly displayed in the lieutenant's face.

'We have him then. In Whitby? In the north? What on earth was he doing up there? Is he still in the place?' The lieutenant looked hopefully at him.

'Yes, as far as I know.' The sergeant raised both eyebrows — however, there is only one way to find out, sir.'

'Do you fancy a journey to the coast, Douglas?'

'I was hoping you would ask me that, sir. For it is the one desire I want eagerly to fulfil.'

'Good man, I shall give you two men, and four days. Find him, silence him and bring me something back to remember him by, like some gold!' He patted the soldier on his shoulder. 'Waste no time, man.'

The lieutenant gave him his signed orders. 'Use these as you see fit and return with only the best of news that the matter has been dealt with finally and completely. Make no mistakes this time, he must not escape again. Now, waste no more time. Four days, then we must move to the coast and make ready for the journey to Spain.'

'Yes, sir.' The sergeant took the paper and left, anxious to pick his two favourite henchmen, both burly Irish soldiers, who would look the other way for a tossed coin. He would relish these orders above all previous ones. Soon, he promised himself, Samuel would say goodnight for the last time.

★ ★ ★

Amelia wrote down the names of the two men concerned in what was a blatant matter of using their positions to profit illegally from contraband and war booty.

She had never been involved in anything so daring before. 'These men are very dangerous, Samuel. What if they find out where you are before Father can help you?'

'There is no way they can, my dear. I have no previous connection with this town and who would think that the Samuel Knight of old would settle to a docile or domesticated existence in such a place as this?'

'What exactly was the 'Samuel of old', like?' Amelia asked pointedly.

'Bold, brash, determined and a survivor, but I hope amidst my many other qualities there was a modicum of decency and honour. But it took me some years to reform from a mud-lark, cutpurse and then escape from the gang

69

that used boys like me to break into large houses, to become the person I am today.'

He was looking at her earnestly and she did not doubt that one word of what he had said was the truth. Her mother would not look at him in the street if she knew about this side of his life, however, her father just might respect him for the man he had reformed into from such derisory beginnings.

'How did you get away from them? Who helped you, Samuel? Surely a child cannot turn away from crime unless he is shown how to by someone more able to help him?' Amy stared at him and he edged nearer to her placing her delicate hand between his two large rough ones.

He had worked his way up from the lowest level of society to a place of respectability, that she could tell. His hands were not soft like some *gentlemen* she had been introduced to.

'I was sent into a bishop's palace, to

rob him of his silver, and was caught red-handed by the man himself. Fortunately he was a compassionate man. Instead of sending me for trial, he took me into his household. He slowly showed me that he was prepared to trust me. He was the first person who ever had. He showed me I could be something different.

'He let me eat with him at his own table, and then, in his vast library he taught me how to read. First English, then French and later Latin. Lovingly, he showed me his collection of maps and explained how to use a sextant. I was fascinated by everything and everyone he spoke of.

'It was then the happiest time of my life. I was to be sent by him to Cambridge. However, he died suddenly, and I was left homeless once more, with nothing but the clothes he had bought me and his books that he had given me, so I began to teach.'

'You are a complete mixture of different lives and experiences all within one short lifetime, Samuel. How did you become a . . . smuggler then?' Amelia was surprised when he laughed at her statement.

'You could have me hanged, Miss Amelia, for what I have disclosed to you already. I have never spoken to another mortal so openly since Bishop Michael used to sit with me in front of the big open fire of the palace, listening for hour upon hour. You are . . . '

'Tell me,' Amy said, squeezing his hand impatiently. She was fascinated by this man who was more interesting than any she had ever met before or read about in her books.

'I was bored with teaching. I wasn't ready to be saddled with a wife and settle down, and besides the headmaster's daughter had fixed her sights firmly on me. She inferred that if I chose to ignore her advances one more time she would tell her father I had acted improperly towards her and my position would be forfeited.' He smiled at Amy as she was literally sitting on the edge of the pew, staring at him wide-eyed.

'So you left?' she asked excitedly.

'Yes, I left. She did not know my true character, or my past. I packed up my things, handed in my notice and moved to London. I was fascinated by both the river and the sea. I wanted to put my navigational skills to the test so I took various jobs, just for the experience, not the money, until I was a proficient seafarer myself, avoiding the navy at all costs.'

Amy looked horrified. 'Why? Would you not fight for your country?'

'Yes, gladly, but not to starve on a poorly equipped ship eating grubby biscuits whilst the officers ate their meat. Nor did I fancy having a flogging for speaking or acting outside of their rule book. No, that was not for me. It was whilst working on a coal ship that I overheard a conversation between the captain and the sergeant.

'It was obvious that they were not talking about government business, but their own illicit trade, and then I saw the opportunity to foil their plans and . . . ' he looked down shame-faced at their entwined hands.

'Secure your future for yourself.' Amelia finished his sentence for him.

He shrugged his shoulders and released her hand. 'I cannot blame you for condemning my actions. I suppose that old habits die hard. But I have vowed to right the wrong they are doing the country and to return their latest catch to the correct authorities.

'They have taken gold from the coffers of our soldiers' pay chest and seized it, blaming a French raid. It was no such thing. They arranged it with their partner in France. I have the gold, but I cannot just walk into a barracks or I shall be arrested for taking it. Your father would know what to do.'

'Then we shall waste no more time. We must send this post-haste, and pray that he is accessible and not months from civilisation.'

She rushed downstairs to rejoin her

sister. Samuel placed the letter in his coat pocket. He would take it straight to the mail-coach.

As they stepped on to the flagstone floor of the porch, neither of them saw Aunt Sarah standing in the shadows behind the stairs, which she too had just descended.

# 6

Amelia returned to Ruth, who blushed slightly as she disturbed their privacy and hastily commentated on James' work. 'Your work should be shown in the London galleries, sir,' she said enthusiastically, and saw a look of pride cross his face.

'Isn't he so very talented, Amelia?' Ruth gushed, as she stared at both him and the painting with admiration.

'Yes, very.' Amy smiled at her sister, she was looking so happy. Amy, however, was bursting with so much information that she was desperate to discuss with her sister, but did not dare to. So she contented herself with sitting down and talking about art, whilst her mind whirled with all that she had learned about Samuel in the previous hour.

Far from scaring her away from him

with his disclosures of his past life, he was becoming more interesting each time she was with him, but what appealed to her the most was that, far from being her Knight in shining armour, it was she who was helping him out of danger.

She liked the idea very much. Life with Samuel Knight would never be dull, as it was with her dear mama.

'Amelia, Ruth, it is time you rejoined your mother for lunch, my dears.'

Sarah's voice surprised both Ruth and Amelia because neither had heard her enter the church or tread upon the cold stone floor.

'Aunt Sarah.' Amelia stood up and welcomed her to show her the painting and Ruth's drawing. Then she turned to her and smiled. 'You are so graceful on your feet, Aunt Sarah, that I didn't hear you enter.'

'No, Amelia, I am not. You didn't hear me enter because I was already in the church when you young people arrived this morning.' Sarah looked directly at Amy, who swallowed and thought hard about how to reply, and what her aunt could be implying.

She glanced at Ruth and James but they were too busy whispering discreet goodbyes as Ruth packed up her sketch box, to have heard her lowered words.

'You were where? In the vestry, seeing to the Reverend's robes, perhaps?' Amy asked optimistically, with a nervous tremor disclosed within her voice.

'No, Amelia. I never see to anyone's robes. I was in the gallery, quietly praying, until my solace was disturbed.' Sarah gave no hint of emotion away.

Amy did not have any idea if Sarah had seen or heard what she and Samuel had said, or of his proposal of marriage or the disclosure of his own past. She just stared blankly at her aunt in an almost silent plea that she would not betray them, or cause Samuel any harm.

Ruth stood by their side. 'Is Mama feeling stronger today?' she asked.

'Your mother has decided to get out of her bed and is dressed. She wishes us all to go into town to find her a warmer coat and some powders to help her sleep, the air should do her good. It is time she ventured out more or she shall never acclimatise to the sea breeze.'

Gale, Amy thought, but did not say anything.

'So please come now,' her aunt continued, 'or else by the time we manage to manoeuvre her out of the house she will have succumbed and gone back to bed.'

Ruth walked towards the door, but Amelia tapped her aunt's shoulder. 'Aunt Sarah, if you have been here since before we arrived, how is it possible you know Mama's state of attire and well-being?'

'Because, my dear, whilst you day-dreamed and chatted to your sister about — whatever, my maid ran up here to me, as instructed, and told me when your mama should show any sign of life this morning. Now, shall we go?'

She turned and joined Ruth. Her manner was terse and put Amelia firmly in her place, giving her mind no peace at all. How would she explain to Samuel, if Sarah decided to expose him? She must speak with her privately at the first opportunity.

★   ★   ★

The opportunity, sadly for Amy, did not arise before they left the house. It was as if Sarah was deliberately placing either Ruth or their mother in between them.

Amelia had all but given up as they entered the milliner's shop in the town.

'Prudence, please make yourself right at home here. Miss Catherine will see to your requirements and Ruth shall give you the benefit of her artistic nature as to what suits you best.' Sarah smiled at Prudence. 'I shall take Amelia to the tea-rooms and, when you two have finished here, please join us there.'

'Yes, that would be splendid, my

dear.' Prudence, happy to be the centre of attention and spending money on clothes, which was her favourite pastime, settled down contentedly on a large chair.

Sarah turned to Amelia. She cupped her hand under her elbow and briskly walked her out of the shop and along a cobbled street, which twisted upwards as it curved around.

'Where are we going, Aunt Sarah?' Amy asked as they were walking at quite a brisk pace.

'To the tea-rooms.' Sarah stopped outside a bay window made of small panes of glass. She was almost marched through the door.

Once inside, Sarah asked to be seated in a little bay, where they could overlook the harbour and watch for Prudence and Ruth to arrive.

Without asking what Amelia preferred to drink Sarah ordered tea and cake for them both, and waited for the waitress to go away before even looking at Amy.

'You, girl, are dabbling in things you do not understand, meddling in lives that are far removed from your own kind, and ultimately dancing with danger. What do you think you are trying to do?'

Sarah kept her voice low, but it was filled with both anger and concern. 'What would happen to you if those evil men that he spoke about found you alone with him. They are soldiers — trained to kill and . . . Well, never mind what else soldiers — bad soldiers — can do. Oh, Amelia, you worry me so. It is a shame that what has been already said and done cannot be undone.'

'Help him,' Amy replied.

'Help him! That's all you can say. Should I send for the militia or the dragoons or perhaps both?' She shook her head in complete dismay.

'What would you do if you were in my place?' Amelia looked at her aunt earnestly and saw her cheeks flush slightly. 'I love him. We are a match for each other. I know we have not known each other for long, Aunt Sarah, but he is so different and he has survived such an abysmal past. Please help him, help us both?'

'I know what I should do. I should go straight to your mama and tell her precisely what games you are up to and of the man's proposal to you — and in a house of God, too!' Sarah looked anxiously around her as her voice had raised slightly more than she had intended it to be.

Content that no-one else had heard her she continued. 'You will bring ruin upon yourself, and your mama could never contend with that. Don't you go running off with this man. Your mama would be finished. She is not strong like we are, she had been mollycoddled into being fairly useless at life's darker moments, as well you are aware.'

Amelia leaned forward. 'You are not telling her are you, though? You have heard all, and yet not uttered a word to my mama, or prevented the letter from being sent to my father. You could have at anytime, but you didn't, so I ask you again . . . What would you do in my place?'

Amy sat back as the tray was brought to them and Sarah quietly regained her composure. She did not answer for a moment or two, but sat thoughtfully turning a silver fork over in her hand.

'He is wrong you know? They will trace him here. This is a small harbour, but people travel from and to here, and through. We have soldiers, sailors and fishermen who go to many ports. It will only be a matter of time before the net tightens on him, and I will not stand by and see you caught in it along with him. Sarah shook her head again. 'Amy, you place me in an unenviable position. What do I do with you?'

'Help me, and help Samuel. You know this town, you have many friends here. The people trust and respect you. Please be his eyes and ears. Warn him if they come looking for him. Let us pray that Father will arrive first. He would be able to sort this whole thing out for us,' Amy said, as she sipped the welcome warm liquid.

'He would sort you out, too!' Sarah answered defiantly.

'You like him, though, don't you?' Amy asked.

'I have always admired your father tremendously. He is a man of action and honour. I pray that he returns safe and in good time.' Sarah ate her cake genteelly.

'I meant, Samuel,' Amelia added.

'I know exactly who you meant. I have given my silence on this matter as confirmation that I am in the belief that what your young man has told you is the God's honest truth. But I will tell you this, Amelia, if I have to choose between helping you or him, I will protect you with every part of my being. Now, enough of your intrigues and you will not use the church as a convenient meeting place for your 'trysts'.'

'Aunt Sarah that is so unfair

. . . where more suitable for a man, who is earnest to propose, I . . . ' Amy saw the determined look on her aunt's face and thought twice about challenging her further. 'Yes, Aunt Sarah, you are quite right. I have behaved improperly.'

'Good girl,' Sarah said, as she removed a crumb from her delicate lip. 'Remember that, as I usually am.'

# 7

The riders arrived by the shadow of the abbey in the depth of the night. The rain beat down upon their greatcoats, but they were undaunted by it because, as soldiers, they were used to inclement weather.

Two of them were not even in their poverty ridden homeland. Instead, they were in England surrounded by people they despised, including the sergeant, but he had one saving grace, other than his rank — he paid them well for their 'extra' duties. Whilst he did so, they would be loyal to him.

'Why aren't we goin' straight to the inn?' one of the men asked his sergeant. He was anxious to conclude the business quickly and then find himself a drink, a woman and a bed for the night.

'We need to know which inn first. It's like a rabbit warren down there and he mustn't slip through our fingers again! Wait till we see the sign, then we go down.' The sergeant dismounted and handed the man the reins of his horse.

The other man looked up at the moonlit abbey ruins and asked, 'Now what sort of sign would that be now?'

'Well it isn't a divine one, that's for sure.' The man chuckled.

Meanwhile, the sergeant had unearthed a bundle wrapped in an oilskin. He handled it carefully because within it was a lamp, which he lit and swung it three times towards the old church down the slope.

Quickly he extinguished it and placed the lamp back exactly where it had been found.

There was a moment's silence whilst they waited for the response and, surely enough, two swings of a lamp was seen in the distance, then a pause, followed by another one.

'Come, men, now we go in, quietly.' They made their way down slowly, but soon the slope became so steep and treacherous that they had to dismount and walk the nervous animals down.

Far from being the quiet unobserved entrance they had anticipated, the animal's hooves and neighing made enough noise to arouse Sarah from her slumber. She watched from the window as the three figures were led down the bank by a figure she recognised only too well — Jacob Bloom!

Sarah ran up two levels and opened the window that overhung the street from the roof. She picked up a small ornamental shell from the window sill and tossed it at the window across the street.

She had known for three days that Amelia and Samuel had used this method to contact each other since their meetings at the church had been disclosed and stopped.

After a few seconds a figure opened the window. 'Amy, do you want me to meet you — now?' He was pulling on his shirt.

'No, sir! I want you to get yourself out of there silently, and come over here!' Sarah spoke just loud enough for him to hear her. 'You have unexpected guests arriving via the steps.'

Like a flash of lightning he was gone. Sarah made her way downstairs and waited for him to make his escape. She knew his type, they were survivors, daring, but often those around them were not so lucky, but she liked him and felt he and Amy were right for one another so she would do her part to help them whilst she could.

★ ★ ★

The three men led by Jacob, tied the animals to the front of the inn, then they entered by the front door. No sooner had they disappeared inside, than Samuel, with his bag and small trunk in his arms ran from the steps by the side of the inn, across the cobbled street and into Sarah's house.

She shut the door quietly and led him up to the attic room. Both tiptoed, neither saying a word until the loft room door was closed safely behind them.

He went to the small window and peered anxiously outside. Nothing seemed to happen for some minutes then he saw movement in the room he had been sleeping in not all that many moments before. He witnessed a few shadows darting across the window, then nothing.

Shortly after, figures were running around the inn, down the steps to the harbour. Up and down the cobbled street they ran, but eventually, with gestures of disgust, they returned to the inn.

Samuel leaned against the wall and faced Sarah.

'I owe you my life, thank you.'

Sarah was touched by the openness and gratitude that he was displaying. He was genuine, of that she was sure.

Sarah could see that he was visibly shaken by his narrow escape. 'Yes, you do. It is in your best interest that nobody but me knows that you are up here — nobody! Do I make myself clear?' Sarah had both hands rested on her hips as she insisted that he agree with her.

'Yes, you do, and for Amelia's sake you are right, but will you tell her that I escaped safely and will be back in touch with her as soon as this mess is cleared up?' He looked at her in earnest.

'I shouldn't, but God forgive me, I will. I shall bring food and water to you and you will stay silent. Once I know the men have gone, you shall be free to move, but they have their spies here. You will not be able to walk these streets freely until they have been reprimanded by the authorities, and when that will be is anyone's guess.'

She looked around the sparse room. It did have a rug on the floor and there was a small table, a chair and not a lot else. 'I'll fetch you up some bedding and comforts, but at least you are alive.'

'I've been in worse places than this, ma'am, much worse, I promise you.' He smiled.

'I don't doubt it, but you're in my home and I always make my guests feel as comfortable as I can.' Sarah paused and looked at him. 'I pray that this will be over for you soon, Mr Knight, for there can be no future for you and Amelia so long as you are a marked man. You see that don't you?'

'Yes, I love her too much to drag her around the streets of London, living in the shadows, never knowing who may creep up from behind when you least expect it.' He looked at the window for a moment, then added, 'What is her father like, ma'am?'

Sarah let out a small chuckle. 'In some ways, I have to admit, he is very like you. I'll fetch you the blankets, but no light. No-one must know that you are here.'

He nodded and Sarah left. If she was honest, she wished also that she was a few years younger herself, then shook her head at such a fanciful notion and admitted it would need to be more than a few.

Amelia awoke early. She couldn't rest and her mind was in perpetual turmoil, so she went for a walk before breakfast. It was not expected of her to do such a reckless thing on her own, but she had had no word from Samuel for two days. She stepped outside. People were already going about their business and the fishing boats had left on the tide.

The church standing before her was empty. The wind was icy cold, but refreshing, unlike the London air.

She breathed in deeply filling her lungs as she stared at the restless sea. She had tossed a small stone at the inn window and an irate woman had shouted abuse back at some boys who were playing in the street.

Samuel had left without saying a solitary word to her. Aunt Sarah had said he would come back when it was safe, but Amy did not know how long that would be. Their mama was already planning the return home. Messages had been sent to ready the house for them as soon as her paying guests, as she referred to them, had left.

She was soon about to have a huge shock delivered to her by Ruth, who was besotted with her young artist friend, James. He was planning to take Ruth, Amelia, and her mama to his parents for dinner that very evening and then on his return make his intentions known to Prudence.

They wanted to marry each other, they were in love and he had money, so her mama should be happy, but Amy knew she was also a very selfish lady and doubted that she would be willing to let both her daughters go at once, or stay in this town. It had not been the place her mama's wild imagination had decided it should be.

# 8

Amy was more troubled by the thought of life without Ruth, devoid of Samuel, that she cared to admit. She walked towards the headland, sheltering momentarily from the wind behind the church.

She wanted to be where she could feel the fresh air against her cheeks and look out at the open sea — how she would miss all of it.

'You really should not come out on your own like this, you never know who you might meet,' the deep voice was now so familiar to her that happiness swept through her like a wave upon the beach.

She moved so that she could see the figure clearly standing in the recess of the wall. 'Samuel! I thought you'd gone. Why are you hiding here?'

'Because they came looking for me

and I'm supposed to be in hiding, but I saw you walk out here and I had to speak to you . . . I couldn't bear to leave without explaining things to you, or holding you one last time.'

He opened his arms and she clung to him, wrapped in his greatcoat, sheltered from the raw elements and, with the warmth of his body against hers, she felt safe and loved.

'Where will you go?' she asked, not really wanting to know unless she could join him.

'I'm not sure . . . ' He looked away from her. 'Amelia, I have no wish to lie to you, but I have friends who would hide me. It is best you do not know who they are, or you will be involved and . . . '

'I am already involved. If that letter falls into the wrong hands then I shall be in as much danger as you yourself.' Amy looked up at his strained face.

'For your own sake, I shall not come near you again until this matter is resolved.' He tried to unwrap her arms from his waist, but she held him firmly, stretching up so that she could kiss his lips.

He responded and they were lost in a private moment of unity and passion to even notice the three men who rode up the steep slope back towards the abbey and the moor road.

When the clatter of hooves striking against stone drifted across to their ears, instantly they sank low down on to their haunches and half crawled around the other side of the church.

'Is that them?' Amy asked.

Samuel nodded, but placed a finger to his mouth. They slipped inside the church and ran up the stairs to the gallery. Once there, they huddled together until the sound of the animals had long gone and they realised they were just content to stay in each other's arms.

'I must go back now, before they return.' Samuel stood up.

'They have gone, Samuel. They might never come back.' Amelia was hopeful.

'I do not believe that anymore than you do. You leave first and I shall follow you when you are out of sight.' He kissed her tenderly. 'Once your father replies then all will be well.'

'How will you know when he does?' Amelia asked and saw that he could not but stifle a grin.

'You are too inquisitive, just trust me and question me no more.' He turned to go.

'You said you saw me walk out here. How?' She saw his smile drop and he turned his back to her as he took a pace towards the stairs.

'You are not still at the inn, yet you are close you will know when father replies . . . Samuel, you are hidden in our aunt's house! Sarah is hiding you, isn't she?' Amy ran to him. 'She was so certain that you would return, because you have never left us.'

He wrapped an arm around her and kissed her firmly on her mouth. 'Amy, I cannot leave you, can I? Now, please go and say nothing of this.'

She ran down the stairs to the outside and returned happily to her aunt's knowing he too would be there as soon as he was able. Amelia did not see him climb on to the roof tops, like he had as a child, and then slip in through a back window of the house. But Sarah did, as she was waiting for him in the attic and she was far from amused at his escapade.

'I thought you would have had more sense, man!' Her voice was filled with anger, but quietly spoken.

'I'm sorry, ma'am, I had to . . . ' Samuel straightened himself. He had removed his coat to climb through the window and leaned out to pull it in after him.

'You had to risk your own neck and my niece's reputation. I tell you it will be your neck that stretches if you do such a thing again. I will protect her at all costs. Now we have had news of Amelia's father. He is expected back within the month, so Prudence is readying herself to return home at the end of this week. Which means you, sir, will have to either stay here or travel as the driver in disguise and await her father's wrath when he eventually makes it home to his estate. However, I shall not let Prudence know you travel with them, but it could be a way of getting you out of this town alive.'

'Do you think her father will help me and approve of me as a prospective son-in-law to his youngest daughter?'

His question was serious, but Sarah laughed and had a fit of coughing as she tried to stifle her laughter. Once she composed herself, she looked at him and shook her head. 'Samuel Knight, if that is your real name . . . '

'It is as real as any I have ever had,' he admitted.

'You do not ask much from life do you?' She looked at him and grinned.

'If you don't ask, you don't find out,' he answered and winked cheekily at her.

'Well you are asking the wrong person, for I am not Amelia's father and I dare say you will have your answer soon enough. Now I must go and remonstrate with my niece, and frighten her into caution.'

'Thank you, ma'am,' he said thoughtfully.

She was so touched by his honesty, but prayed she would not have to break his trust in her in order to save the respect of Amelia.

She came down the stairs as a firm knock sounded on her door. She straightened her bonnet and skirts before opening it, then stepped back in awe as she saw a face from the past.

'My how the world is suddenly full of surprises. Come in, Archibald. We weren't expecting you so soon.'

Sarah stepped back as the tall broad figure entered, his skin tanned, hair long and held by a leather at the nape of the neck. He removed his hat, kissed her cheeks and gave her a hug that took the wind from her lungs.

'Where're my girls and what's this nonsense Amelia's writing to me about?'

Sarah regained her composure and whispered into his ear, 'Not nonsense, as well you know, it's trouble Archie and you are the one who has to sort it out!'

He looked down on her, eyes wild as ever they were. 'Not before I break the neck of the blackguard who has got my baby writing notes to me that could have her murdered if they got into the wrong hands.

'If I find him I'll beat him to within an inch of his life before I ask him his part in this subterfuge. Now, where's me beautiful Ruth?'

'Father!' Ruth ran into his arms. 'Oh, Mama will be so pleased to see you. I must tell her you are here.' She ran up to Prudence's room.

Archibald looked at Sarah. 'Why didn't I marry the sister who had a brain inside her head, eh?' He smiled at her and placed an arm around her shoulders.

'Because I was already happily wed.' Sarah looked up at him and he laughed.

'More's the pity,' he said, and walked into the parlour. 'A cup of tea would be appreciated.'

'Hello, Father.' Amelia's voice made him stop in his tracks and stare at her. 'I'm so glad you are here.'

'You, girl, are . . . '

'Oh, Archibald! My dear husband, why did you not tell us you were arriving. We could have prepared for you.' Prudence pushed past Amelia, but her father's eyes remained firmly fixed on hers.

'Don't worry, my dear. Instead I have come prepared for you.'

Amelia smiled, but her father did not, and she could feel a knot inside her forming where her stomach usually was.

'I'll help Aunt Sarah to make arrangements.' She left the parlour and made her way to the stairs. She was on the first landing before Sarah caught her skirt and stopped her.

'Oh, no you don't my girl! You stay down here and await your father's

pleasure. I'll not have murder commit-
ted in my home and if you don't handle
this well, that is what will happen. Do
you hear me?'

'Yes, but . . . ' Amy began to reason
with her.

'But nothing!' Sarah would not let
go, she was determined. 'Downstairs,
now!'

'Yes, Aunt.' Slowly, reluctantly, Amy
returned to the parlour, where her
father listened to the small talk of his
wife and stared at Amy relentlessly, and
she returned his every look with a
pleasant confident smile, hoping her
trembling knees were not detectable
under her skirts.

# 9

Amelia watched her father discreetly throughout dinner and tried to judge if he was angry with her or not. Perhaps, she thought, he looked concerned about her in some way, or it could be her imagination. Her note might have crossed with him as he was returning and he had not yet received it.

The latter was highly unlikely, she reasoned, because although he was being his usual jovial self with Prudence and Ruth, he kept side-glancing at her, making her feel extremely ill at ease.

When at last Prudence said she must retire and Ruth left the room with her mama, Amy stood up and immediately offered to help them.

'No,' Sarah said, without hesitation, 'I shall have to arrange the sleeping arrangements to include Archibald, so I shall go with them. You stay here awhile and talk to your father.'

Amelia glared at Sarah, but her silent protest was completely ignored.

'Do you wish a nightcap bringing to you, Archibald?' Sarah asked.

'No, lass. I shall be going out shortly and I'll have one then. Shut the door behind you, woman, whilst I talk to my daughter and find out what the lass has been up to.'

Sarah looked at her, eyes filled with concern, but she closed the door.

Amelia tried to remove the tense atmosphere by smiling at her father. 'So tell me, Father, what adventures you have been on this time. You are looking very well and . . . '

'Sit down, Amy, and don't give me any of your nonsense. You may fool your mama with yer antics but not me, nor Sarah for that matter. Fortunately she was blessed with a rare amount of intelligence for a woman. In fact, I believe she was granted your mother's portion, too. She managed to use her wit and cunning to get an urgent message to me. So tell me, girl, what is this all about?' He removed the intercepted letter from his pocket.

'Mr Knight is a respectable man who needs your help.' She paused whilst her father stared at the ceiling for a moment. She ignored him and continued, 'Samuel is a good man, Father, and these men who are after him are pure evil!'

She raised her voice at the end of the sentence, which instantly brought his attention back firmly on her. For a moment they both stared defiantly at the other.

Archibald took her hand in his own. 'My dear girl, you are innocent . . . ' He paused for a moment and looked her straight in her eyes, adding, 'I hope?'

'Father, of course I am!' Amy was shocked that he may think she had acted without propriety, then her cheeks flushed slightly as she remembered the feeling of Samuel's body against her own when they had so tenderly embraced.

'Good, so you should be. I shall not have your reputation tarnished by a rogue and an opportunist.' Archibald stopped as Amy pulled her hand from his.

'Sam . . . Mr Knight is neither of those. He is a man who was born into hardship — on the wrong side of society, who with the help and blessing of a bishop, saved his own soul from the living hell he had been born into.' Amelia's face was flushed as she defended Samuel with utter passion.

'You have 'his' word on all of this I take it and nothing else?' Archibald stared at her and she was filled with the frustration of knowing that there was nothing she could produce as proof that what she had said was correct and not a lie.

The door opened slowly and Samuel stepped into the room. Amy looked at these two men. They were of a height and, she felt, an equal match in their character for each other.

'You have my word, sir, for what that

may be worth. I can give you dates, names, and the details of my past for you to confirm at a later date, but right now all I can do is offer myself for you to make up your own mind as to my integrity and honour.' Samuel stepped farther inside the parlour followed by Sarah who closed the door again behind them.

'I should call you out, lad, for risking my daughter's safety in trying to save your own skin!' He waved the note in Samuel's face.

Samuel did not flinch. He stared beyond the paper to the man who held it. 'I could not blame you if you did, but neither would I offer any defence.'

'Father, I insisted that I . . . we could help him.'

Her father looked at her and raised an eyebrow. 'Who did you want to help him?' he asked.

'I wanted you to, but I knew I could help by intervening,' Amy interrupted, but both men's eyes were locked upon each other's.

'No, you interfered in matters that a young lady should not even have knowledge of.' Her father was adamant.

'Amelia, your father is quite right. I should never have allowed you to become involved in my own mess. I was being selfish. I wanted to be free of this situation so that if we stood any chance of having a future together our path would be made clear, but my love for you obscured my better judgement.'

Amy saw her father's eyebrows and colour both rise.

'I didn't stop to think how far the rot of the operation could have gone.' Samuel was serious. There was obviously no hypocrisy held within his words.

'Now you have,' Archibald answered. 'You, sir, have a nerve, of that there is no doubt. As to your honour, that I have yet to fathom and regarding my daughter's future . . . ' he sighed as he saw the pleading look Amy gave him, ' . . . will lie beyond this mess and possibly you. Firstly, we must speak honestly together. Sarah, take Amelia to her mama and sister. You, sir, can explain to me, and I am no naïve maid so do not try to hoodwink me, man, or your head will not remain long on your shoulders.'

Her father looked at her and said, 'Go! And make no more interference in men's work, do you hear me, woman?' His last comment was addressed equally to Sarah as well as to her.

'Father, how did you return so swiftly from Spain?' Amy asked before Sarah could be ushered out of the room.

'I obviously was not in Spain!' He pointed to the door.

Amy looked at Sarah, but her aunt took hold of her arm and steered her through the door. Both women left the room with an air of defiance.

'You have no criminal record, man, but that I believe is more by stealth and luck than by justice. You have been stretching your good fortune to the limit! So what do you have to say for yourself?'

Archibald was standing square in front of Samuel who had decided the best way to handle the man was to meet him with equal but polite force.

'I turned from crime as a boy, as I explained to Amelia, with the help of a truly good man. I have taken advantage of certain opportunities since then and have outwitted the Revenue services on occasion.'

'That would not take a lot of acumen to do.' Archibald laughed then sat down by the fire. 'Continue.'

'However, I intercepted the operation of a certain lieutenant and sergeant whilst working along the Thames. I had intended to hand in the chest. However, I started thinking.'

'What you could do with the lovely gold, if you just kept it?' Archibald was watching him closely, but Samuel remained standing in the parlour and looked at him.

'No, I have been successful enough without taking the pay of men who are at war. I realised I could not just go into a garrison or a government office with it and start accusing the officers without proof of any kind. They could so easily turn it around and frame me.'

'So you came here?' Archibald asked.

'No, that was an accident, but I had not planned my next move before I met Miss Amelia and your good family. I could not have planned that.'

'However, you are an opportunist,' Archibald said accusingly.

'I cannot blame you for thinking that is what I am doing, but sir, it is not. I want the money to go to where it belongs, in the soldiers' pockets. I want the vermin who took it from them and blamed the French brought to justice, and I would dearly like to marry your daughter and provide for her.'

'By hell, man, you don't want much do you?' Archibald stood up and buttoned his waistcoat. 'Do you think the government is a fool? Do you think they would not become suspicious that the French are managing to intercept our gold without smelling a rat or two?

What is a fortune to you and them is not to the French government. However, it was sufficient to annoy and frustrate my superiors. You go back to your attic.' He smiled at Samuel's surprise that he was fully aware of where he had been. 'I am an intelligence officer, I am paid to know things.'

'What will you do, sir?' Samuel asked.

'I shall find your pursuers and reintroduce them to the army. You stay out of sight and I shall deal with you later. Tell me, man, why are you not fighting for your country?' Archibald stared at him.

'I have had a problem adhering to strict, unnecessary rules.' Samuel was being honest.

'Oh, the army would break you of that.'

'I know, that is why I am not in the army, sir.' He opened the door.

'Perhaps, Knight, your talents could be better used other than in the rank and file.' Archibald dismissed him with a gesture of his hand.

* ★ ★

The three men returned to the inn that night, exhausted that they had not uncovered any sign nor the trail of their man. Douglas knew that if he returned to the lieutenant the next day without him all hell would break out and his officer would take out his frustration on him.

As they entered the bar, he noticed a large man seated on a stool overlooking the harbour. He looked like a sailor, from his tanned weather worn face. His grey hair was tied neatly at the nape of his neck and he sucked repeatedly on his clay pipe.

'Good day to you, sirs.' The man's voice was rough but confident.

'Is it?' Douglas said sarcastically, and walked over to the stranger. 'I hadn't noticed.'

His two associates sat down at the bar and ordered their ale.

'You a local man?' he asked.

Archibald looked up at him. He was

in no doubt that this was the sergeant in question. 'Aye, I live across the way.'

The sergeant looked back to the innkeeper. 'Two jugs of ale over here,' he shouted.

'That's uncommonly decent of you. Is there something you'd be wantin' in return, sir, or are you just a charitable gent?' Archibald accepted the ale, but kept his eyes firmly on the man who had offered it to him.

'Not a lot, sir, just a little of your time and possibly some information.' He pulled up a chair and made himself comfortable.

'We have to be leaving here soon and you see we haven't found our friend. We came here looking for him but no-one seems to know where he is staying. Perhaps you could help us to find him.' The man raised his jug of ale and smiled, but his eyes remained hard and impassive.

Archibald looked at the man's unshaven and scarred face and wondered who on earth his spirited daughter, Amelia, had got herself involved with. 'What is his name?' Archibald continued as if in ignorance of who they were.

He wanted to find out what they knew first before he had them rounded up, but not here, so near to his own family. No, he would lure them away from the area first.

'He was lost at sea in his boat. The boat was bought here, but we haven't found our dear Samuel.' The man shook his head then looked up at Archibald, 'Samuel Knight, that's his name, tall like yourself.'

Archibald grinned broadly. 'Aye, well I'm not surprised you haven't found him here. He's staying over at the Black Sheep over on the moor road. He's been there a few weeks now. Quite a friendly sort for a stranger.' Archibald supped his ale.

'Can you take us there?' The sergeant stood up.

'What, now?' Archibald asked as if totally shocked at the idea.

'Yes, now and I'll pay you well for your trouble. Come, man, we have to leave tomorrow.'

'Well, all right, but I have not got a horse.'

'No need to worry, we'll find one for you.' He signalled to one of his men who quickly went finding a horse for Archibald.

Within minutes they were all mounted upon the animals and headed out to the moor road. As soon as they left, Jacob Kell followed on his own horse at a discreet distance.

*  *  *

Sarah ran up the stairs to the attic. 'Samuel, you have to follow them. They have Jacob scouting for the first sign of trouble. You've got to get him before he can warn them that they are headed for an ambush.' Sarah's face was full of panic. 'Don't kill him, though, or you'll swing.'

Samuel had been wearing his coat

and was all ready to go at the first sign of trouble. He gave Sarah a comforting pat on her shoulder as he descended the stairs.

'Take Archibald's horse, Samuel. It's all ready in the yard.'

Samuel nodded and left swiftly and without sound. Sarah sat back down on the stairs and prayed.

# 10

Samuel left the yard and walked the horse through the narrow streets. Its hooves were covered in cloths so as to deaden the sound. Once away from the town he removed them and rode at speed towards the moor road. Samuel was a survivor.

He had grown up with the need of an extra sense that warned him when he was being followed. He realised someone was tracking him, so he pulled his pistol from under his coat and readied it to fire if necessary.

'Samuel, Samuel, it is I, James!' the familiar voice drifted across the night air to greet him.

'Dear God, man! I could have put a hole straight through you,' Samuel exclaimed.

The man came alongside him sporting a rifle over one shoulder and another on a holster on his saddle.

'Whatever you are doing here? Don't tell me you knew about all of this trouble, and Archibald,' Samuel said as he kicked his horse onwards. He could not believe for one moment that Amelia would divulge such secrets to him, or her sister. She would be far too protective of Ruth.

'There aren't many in town that don't know you have been holing up in Sarah's house. It's one of Archibald's safe houses. Don't forget this is a very busy harbour town, but small. Not a lot happens within it that the locals do not learn about,' James explained as if that would be sufficient for him to understand all.

'So why did nobody tell the three men who have been looking for me where I was?' Samuel asked.

'Simply because they were strangers, and folk around here don't trust them.' James smiled at him then directed his horse off the main road and on to a narrow track.

Samuel followed a little apprehensively. 'I, too, am a stranger here, or have you forgotten that?' he replied, looking anxiously around him at the boggy ground at the side of the track.

'True, but Sarah isn't. She is very well respected here, as was her husband and as is Archibald. So you have their protection.' James took great care picking his way along. 'Besides, I haven't seen you with Amelia.'

'Really, I thought you were too engrossed with Ruth.' Samuel saw the man turn in his saddle and glance back at him.

'An artist is very observant,' he answered smugly.

'Is this a short cut?' Samuel asked.

'Of course, you can't sneak up on Jacob Kell on the main road. You'd get your brains blown out.' James chuckled at the thought.

'Did Sarah send you?' Samuel asked curiously.

'No, Archibald did because he knew you'd follow him and try to be a hero to impress your darling Amelia.'

'Do you work for Archibald?' Samuel repeated his question.

'I help the war effort where I can through the company, and I draw things.'

'Like faces and maps? People involved in the passing trade,' Samuel commented as he had often seen James down by the harbour drawing.

'Yes, it is what I am good at and it is very rewarding,' James replied and then took another fork in the track and headed for drier firmer land. 'When we get behind that burial mound we shall dismount and approach the inn on foot, if necessary. The dragoons should arrive here shortly. Archibald sent word on ahead.

'Burial mound?' Samuel said, not much caring for the idea of hiding behind one.

'It's an ancient mound, no-one knows who put it there, but no-one has ever come to harm there either, so don't worry. You need to care about the living, not the dead.'

'I'm not scared of ghosts, but I haven't seen a burial mound before, that's all.' Samuel followed in silence.

The mound looked like a small hillock, so Samuel told himself that that was all it was. He did not care for superstition, but as a child he had been made to hide in a graveyard and pass on stolen goods to a fence. It had left him with a fear he had fought throughout his adult life.

They dismounted and secured the horses. 'Can you use one of these?' James asked and held out the spare rifle to Samuel.

'Yes,' he answered confidently, as he had been taught by an old rifleman and prided himself on being a good shot with one.

'Good, follow me but keep low.' James led the way.

He followed, grateful that James was there as he realised he might need back-up in order to outwit these rogues.

'We shall enter via the cellar and

listen to what is happening. If anything goes wrong we shall have to rescue Archibald ourselves, but wait for my instruction — no cavalier acts on your own. I don't want to have to break a young maid's heart by informing her that her true love died a hero.

'The dragoons should be here already. Something isn't right, Samuel. Let's get in there and find out what is.' James scurried around the back of the inn towards the loading door.

Samuel followed warily. They entered through a half door at the back of the stone building. It was used to roll barrels into a cellar room beneath the inn's dispensary.

Fortunately, there was room for them to crawl in and over the top of the stored ale. They could see through a crack in the partly-panelled floor by the dispensary counter and heard raised voices within the parlour above them.

The innkeeper sounded nervous. 'I tell yer 'e was 'ere but 'e's not 'ere now!' His voice gained confidence as he tried to stress the point. However, the three men must have been getting desperate because they were not accepting his answer.

'Hey, ease up, lads. Benjamin is telling yer all he can. He wouldn't lie to Archie, would yer?' Archibald's voice, heavy with accent, was heard trying to pacify them but they were not responding to him. Their actions were becoming more threatening.

'Something's gone wrong, Sam,' James said. 'The message should have brought the dragoons here by now. This isn't going well at all.' James fidgeted, his hand tightening on the rifle.

They heard the sound of heavy wood moving and knew the outside door had been opened. James's face lit up with a moment of optimism but it was short lived.

'This is a set-up, gents. Old Archie here has sent this note for the troops only it didn't reach them.' Jacob Kell's voice echoed around the silent room as his words were heard by the irate men.

'Don't pull that pistol out from your coat, man, or it will be the last thing that you do pull ever again,' the sergeant's voice bellowed as his two henchmen's footsteps could be heard rushing him.

'Who is he?' the sergeant asked Kell.

'I know he's army, but what within it, I don't know. He's related to the woman across the street from the inn.' Jacob's voice trailed off as the sergeant slammed something down hard on a table.

'He's led us on a wild goose chase. That's where Knight is or was. By God, I've rarely been duped in my life but you, sir, have pulled the wool firm over my eyes. Take him outside, give him a good kickin' and then we'll see if his family is prepared to shelter Knight when they see what is left of him.'

James turned to Samuel to say they must rescue Archibald first, but Samuel had left without sound or trace. James swore to himself and prayed the man was not a feckless coward who had deserted them to their fate.

Outside, Samuel skirted around by the shadows of the inn. He waited for them to throw Archibald out. The burly figure rolled across the frosted ground. He stood instantly, ready to retaliate, but the two men had pistols pointed at him.

Jacob had stayed inside to tell the sergeant all he knew about Sarah and her guests, whilst he drank the man's ale.

One man gave his pistol to the other. 'Dermid, hold this,' he said as he bent down and picked up a long narrow log and swung it wide in the air. 'Cover me whilst I soften him up a little.'

The man sneered and took steps towards the trapped Archibald. If he retaliated he could be shot, if he didn't he'd get a beating. So intent were they on watching their victim, neither saw the figure behind them lift the equally lethal log from the discarded pile.

Without hesitation, Samuel brought

it down in one powerful swoop on the man who held the pistols. As he fell to the ground one gun went off narrowly missing Archibald as he pounced upon the surprised soldier. He needed no log. With his bare hands he wrestled the man to the ground and knocked him unconscious by slamming his head against the ice-cold earth.

Jacob Kell burst forward from the inn, but James had him within the sights of his pistol and the man stood stock still dropping his weapon.

Then all three heard the galloping of the sergeant's horse as he made off along the road.

Samuel ran for his horse. He would get him and bring the blackguard back before he could do Amelia or her family any harm. With the rifle thrown by its strap across his shoulder, he raced off into the distance, leaving Archibald to follow and James to tie up the men and leave them secure at the inn whilst he fetched the dragoons himself.

* * *

Amelia awoke in the depth of the night. She couldn't explain why, but she felt restless. She decided to take a great risk and tiptoed up the stairs to the attic. Slowly she opened the door, a stair creaked and she stopped, frozen to the spot. 'It's only me Samuel?' she said calmly but quietly.

'Good,' replied Samuel's slightly muffled voice. She quickly ran up the last few stairs. The attic window was open, making the room very chilly.

By the window stood a man who was not as tall as Samuel, he was older and wore a soldier's uniform. A greatcoat was thrown on Samuel's makeshift bed. In his hand he held a pistol.

'Who are you?' Amelia wrapped her shawl around her tightly, suddenly she was aware that she was standing in her nightdress before this man with her hair not even bound or capped but loose over her shoulders.

'I'm Samuel's friend. He sent me to

fetch you to him. He wants . . . you.' He looked her up and down as the moonlight silhouetted her figure. 'He wants you to come with me and meet him on the road. He is going to take you away to elope. Romantic or what, eh? So you come with me with no fuss, now and I'll show you where he is holed up.'

Amelia's mind was racing. This must be one of the soldiers she wrote to her father about. So where was Samuel and her father? 'Wait here and I'll dress quickly.' She smiled and turned to go but she heard a click as the pistol was raised to point at her.

'There'll be no need for that. You can come with Dougie just as you are. Samuel has shared so many of my possessions he won't mind if for once I share his. He owes me, you see,' he walked over to her, keeping the pistol out of her reach.

Samuel suddenly dropped through the window taking the sergeant by surprise.

Amelia stood still as the men fought together. They made enough noise to wake up the neighbourhood. Eventually Samuel delivered the last blow that stunned the sergeant into silence.

Amelia helped to secure the unconscious figure and lock up the attic firmly until her father returned.

Samuel held her to him. 'Go downstairs and tell your aunt that Archibald will be returning soon. I will wait here until he does.'

# 11

Amelia dressed and waited for the man
to be arrested and taken away. Then she
sat patiently in the parlour until
Samuel, James and her father returned
to the house, tired and cold.

'Father.' She smiled at him, but he
did not smile back.

'Daughter,' he replied solemnly.

'Can we talk now?' she asked
nervously.

'No, I want my bed and so do these
fine men.' He gestured for them to go.
James bid a polite goodbye and left.

Samuel went to speak to them, but
Archibald turned around and faced
him. 'Go to your room man. I have had
enough for this night. You brought
those men to my family home. Tomorrow you will leave!'

'No, Father, please!' Amelia exclaimed
in despair.

'Yes, my girl. On this I will not be moved. Good day, sir!' Archibald appeared to be in a barely controlled fury.

Samuel had no option but to nod his agreement and leave. Amelia tried to run after him, but Archibald held her arm firmly. 'No, my girl, you stay here! No daughter of mine runs after a man!' His voice and his manner adamant.

There was no moving him. Amelia just stared blankly at the door until her aunt appeared.

'Sarah, take her to her room and lock her in if necessary. She will not leave it until our guest has left in the morning — not under any circumstance.'

Amelia was going to protest one last time but her aunt shook her head and she knew that her cause was lost.

⋆ ⋆ ⋆

Amelia couldn't sleep. She dressed and packed her bag with a few essential belongings.

'What do you think you are doing?' Ruth rubbed her eyes and sat up in her narrow bed.

'I shall make myself ready for when Samuel comes for me.' Amelia looked out of the window into the night. Moonlight glistened on the distant waves but there was no sign of anyone amongst the shadows of the buildings surrounding the house.

'Think what you are saying, Amelia.' If you step one foot outside this house at night in the company of a man, your reputation will be ruined and you shall be disowned by Father and I shall never see you again!' Her voice trailed off and she clung to her blanket as her moist eyes stared imploringly at Amelia.

'Oh, Ruth, I don't know what to do!' She sat beside her sister on the bed and held her hand in hers. 'I cannot imagine he would leave so easily and accept Father's order without question. It is too much. We love one another, I do not wish to go back to life without him.' Amelia returned to the window and stared out into the dark, watching for any sign of movement at all.

'Amy, you are young . . . there will be others . . . ' her voice was hesitant. 'He is the first man who has paid you personal attention.'

'Like James and you, do you mean?' Amy glanced back at her. 'Has Father given his blessing to you both?'

'No, not yet. Well, I mean he hasn't had time to talk to him yet. That's different, anyway. James has a family and position, unlike Samuel. I mean, he is pleasant enough, but hardly your social equal.' Ruth was bracing herself for Amelia's rebuke but it did not come.

Amy was not paying much attention to her sister. She had seen a figure move in the street below, a tall one wearing a greatcoat and she knew instantly that it was Samuel. He had come for her.

She decided she would give a sign, bring the lamp to the window or something but, before she could act, another figure joined him and she watched silently in stunned disbelief. Her father, unmistakable by his figure and gait. They walked together down the cobbled street. Amy moved swiftly towards the door, leaving her bag on her bed.

'Amy, you're not still going are you? Not after all I have said, surely not?' Ruth grabbed her sister's skirts in a desperate act.

'No, silly! My bag is there isn't it. I'm going to see Aunt Sarah. Back in a moment. You go to sleep before you wake up Mama.' Amy smiled and left before her sister could protest further.

Amy ran down the stairs as quickly as she could. She slid back the bolt on the inside of the door and, slipping quietly outside, ran up the street as quickly as she could.

A dog barked wildly at her from behind a wooded gate. It charged the obstruction but the gate was secured soundly much to Amy's great relief.

# 12

Amy's heart leaped in her chest, but she continued on her way. The cold air bit into her cheeks and the water lapped at the harbour walls. Ahead of her the two figures had disappeared into the darkness, but a carriage was waiting at the end of the street.

Suddenly she was aware that she was very alone, outside at a time of day that she had never been exposed to before. Each shadow held fear for her, every cat that mewed made her jump. The cold was more intense than it had been earlier in the day and every building and alley appeared to be filled with menace.

Wild tales of witches and hobgoblins haunted her, but she wrestled to push all that to the back of her mind and concentrate on the matter at hand — finding Samuel. Amy felt fear like she had never known before. She was alone, and it felt very frightening.

Suddenly a hand grabbed her shoulder. She squealed, and another hand covered her mouth. She kicked out and heard a man swear and curse at her, but the voice was muffled, she was spun around, lifted off the ground and slung over a shoulder before being bundled into the carriage and dumped unceremoniously on the hard floor. Instantly it moved off at great speed.

Amy fought to regain her posture and sat up staring at the man on the seat next to her. She was furious, scared and when she looked up at her father's irate face Amelia stared defiantly back.

'What do you think you are doing?' Her father grabbed her arm and helped her to sit on to the seat. 'Can you not see I have your safety first and foremost in mind?'

'Then why play games with me? Samuel is riding atop, isn't he? You had no intention of turning him away.

Instead you play out a charade in order that I take to my bed like a . . . '

'Like an obedient daughter!' He shouted his words as the coach rattled and shook on its way.

'Why couldn't you trust me with the truth? I am not stupid, Father!' Amy shouted back.

'That is open for interpretation. You have no business interfering in danger-ous issues. If we were not racing against time I should have you returned to your mama and have her lock the door on you. You are determined to ruin yourself.'

'How so, I merely take a ride with my father who is given to unpredictable habits and does not adhere to polite society's rules of behaviour. So why should you take a moonlight trip across the moors, Father?'

'You, girl, should have been sent away from your dim-witted mother and taught some discipline, manners and married off to some poor unsuspecting banker in the city.' He folded his arms and stared at his dishevelled daughter's indignant face.

'I have no wish to be married off,' she protested.

'Haven't you, my girl?' He glanced up at the roof of the carriage and she blushed as he knew how she felt about Samuel. 'Never mind that now. If I had time I would have returned you to safety, but we have a bigger fish to catch and need to be in London before day-break, so you, my girl, are in for a very uncomfortable night and your dear mama, Aunt Sarah and sister are going to have a horrid shock to deal with when you are not found in the morning.

'You will cause them much pain and grief because of your selfish and thoughtless actions.' His voice was no longer so angry but she still stared defiantly at him although his words caused her pain; she had never intended to hurt anyone, just find Samuel.

'Those evil men have been arrested so why did you not retire to bed?' she asked, as the coach lurched over a bump and she lifted off the seat only to crash back down with a thump.

'Because we have no proof against a man who is behind this business, but with Samuel as bait, we can nail him.' Her father smiled at the notion for the first time.

'You would use Samuel as bait?' Amelia exclaimed. 'He could get hurt.'

'Yes, and so could you if you get in our way. We will leave you safe at the gatehouse and you will stay there, not moving from whence we placed you. Then we can finish this business and I can return to France.'

He wagged a finger at her. 'And you will not shame yourself or your mama further. If that man,' he pointed to the ceiling referring to Samuel, 'is half the man I think he is, you will wed him to save your name and then he will return with me and do his part for his King and country, whilst you await his return like a good and noble wife.'

Amelia's face broke into a broad smile and she almost threw herself into her father's arms. He was instantly ill at ease. He was not given to great displays of emotions and he quickly returned her to her seat, but she laughed with relief and humour as she saw his discomfort.

'I thought you were working in Spain?' Amelia asked.

'Well, that is just as well. I have been working in France for some months and the antics of Mr Samuel Knight have come repeatedly to my attention as had the antics of his pursuers. He may have foiled their plans to abscond with the King's gold, but in the process he messed up my plans too.

'We have been trying to tighten the net on the blackguards. Then James sent word that your dear mama had actually made a decision — as usual a very bad one — and my family had been moved to Sarah's for the season. What on earth that woman was thinking about I dread to think.'

'She wanted to marry us off to the local gentry instead of competing with our neighbours for the London gentleman who had far too many richer maids to choose from.'

Amelia laughed as he held his head in his hands in a gesture of mock despair.

'So she found you a 'would be' smuggler and opportunist who was bred on the streets, and Ruth a wealthy young adventurer who is a dab hand with a paintbrush.' He shook his head and leaned back on the seat.

'Then she did well then. You should be grateful to her inspired decision making.' He laughed for a moment, then said solemnly, 'Get what rest you can, girl. Tonight is no joke and you should not be with us.'

She closed her eyes. She was tired but could hardly sleep; instead she imagined what life with Samuel would be like once they were wed.

\*    \*    \*

By the time they had reached their destination, the noise, sights and smells were so very different to either her country home or the fresh smell of the sea.

They pulled into a courtyard of an inn that was directly opposite a barracks. Samuel climbed down. He was wet and cold. Amelia smiled at his tired face as he opened the coach door, but he did not smile back at her.

'What do we do with her, sir?' he asked, hardly looking at her.

Amy was quite hurt, but realised she had acted rashly and endangered them by interfering in their mission, instead of trusting them to return when they had finished. But her father had tried to trick her instead of being honest, and that was not right either.

'Rent the best room they have for her for the one day and night, tell them Mr Brooks will pay the bill.' Archibald spoke to him as if he was his senior officer and Samuel nodded obediently, entering the inn without even glancing back at her.

'Listen, Amelia, you must stay here. I need you to be safe. Do not leave the room. This is a safe house. Food will be brought to you but you will be stopped from leaving until I return, or a message is sent.'

Samuel returned. 'Top floor,' was all he said.

'Fine,' her father answered, as a man appeared in the doorway. 'Keep this lady safe, Benjamin.'

'Father . . . ' Amy looked from her father to Samuel, but they both said in unity — 'Go.'

Amy had to follow the stranger to a small, lonely bedchamber and accept that she now had no choice but to wait.

# 13

Archibald turned to Samuel. 'What we are about to do could backfire on us, are you sure you are willing to go through with it?'

Samuel knew that his life was about to change forever, but then it had changed a number of times in the past so he accepted the opportunity with relish. For each change had led him on to better things and, as he glanced up at the stairs that Amelia had climbed, he smiled and nodded. 'I'm sure. We'll trap the scoundrel and close the net on the lieutenant. It is time we knew how far the rot has spread.'

Archibald gave Samuel a length of narrow rope. Samuel twisted it around his wrists as if he had his hands bound. Archibald then lifted up Samuel's small trunk. He then pulled his pistol out and walked Samuel over at gunpoint to the barracks gatehouse.

'Soldier, tell Lieutenant Spears that there is a man to see him with a Mr Knight, and something that he believes belongs to him.' Archibald stood at the gatehouse whilst a man was sent with his message. Once that man was despatched, Archibald gave a sealed order addressed to Captain Williams to the guard.

The man looked at him as if he did not know what to do. 'I should have sent this to the lieutenant.' He looked perplexed as he realised it was important.

'No, that, lad, you don't do. Wake the good captain and give him that personally and help him to make swift progress to the lieutenant. That is an order of the highest importance — do not give it to any other mortal soul.'

He ordered a soldier to take his place and acted immediately by taking the order off in a different direction to the first messenger.

Samuel took in every detail of the

scene around him. Soldiers were busy going about their duties. They looked at him with equal distrust.

The messenger came back and escorted them to the captain's office. Archibald led Samuel inside.

A tall slim young officer was standing by the window. There was no one else there.

'Samuel Knight, we meet at last.' He stared at Archibald. 'Who are you, man?' he snapped out his question angrily.

'I am your saviour who is just about to save your skin, sir, as your three men celebrated their good fortune too early and let him and this . . . ' he slammed the trunk down on the table, 'slip through their grip. They are now serving a night in a lock up, for their unruly behaviour. However, Douglas and me, we go back a long way. So for a piece of the action and to get this blackguard off my tail, I offered to assist him in their quest, as if were.'

'The key?' The lieutenant viewed the

150

small trunk greedily.

Archie reached inside his pocket and tossed it over to the man.

He opened it and fingered the gold. 'Who else knows of this?'

'No-one,' Archibald answered.

'Except the men who are fighting without pay,' Samuel said. His sarcasm was instantly greeted with a stinging slap across the face from the lieutenant. Samuel held the rope tightly, resisting the urge to floor the man, but he could not do that until they had discovered if his captain was also involved.

The lieutenant counted out some coins and handed them to Archibald. 'You have done well, my man. Take a room at the inn opposite and we shall talk later, when my incompetent sergeant returns.'

Archibald turned the gold over in his fingers before pocketing them. 'What about him?' He nudged Samuel with the pistol barrel.

The lieutenant smiled broadly. 'I'll see he is accommodated in a manner befitting his status. He walked to the door and opened it. 'Guard!' he shouted.

Samuel glanced at Archibald with more than a hint of nervousness. The young officer returned to the trunk and leaned his back against it before the guard entered the room. 'Take this man down to the cells. Have him securely restrained.'

Samuel was pushed towards the doorway, but the figure of Captain Williams, looking quite dishevelled as if he had recently alighted from his bed, blocked the exit.

The lieutenant's composure changed immediately as he straightened and stood to attention.

'What is the meaning of this?' the captain commanded as he approached his desk. He stared at the trunk.

'Sir, remove your belongings this instant. I apologise, sir. This man,' he pointed to Archibald, 'has done us a great service by bringing in a known and wanted smuggler. He has frustrated our missions with his privateering and is a drain on the war effort as well as a coward.' The lieutenant stood pointing at Samuel.

Archibald nodded in agreement, but it was not at the lieutenant, it was at Samuel who was unwrapping the rope from his wrists. They had their answer. The guard looked around confused.

'Guard, you are arresting the wrong man. Seize the lieutenant and take him to the cells until I can bear to look upon him again.' the captain glared at the young officer.

'Sir, you do not understand. This man came in here with a loaded gun, a smuggler and this small trunk. I . . . ' he edged towards the door but Archibald pointed his pistol at him. The man stopped and was joined by two more guards at the door.

'You, sir, are a disgrace to your uniform, your family and your country. Take him out of my sight!'

# 14

The captain stared at Samuel and then Archibald. 'You have lost me my sleep, a sergeant and an officer just as we are about to leave for service on the continent. You have greatly inconvenienced me. However, I dare say that you have done the country a noble service, and as for this blackguard, can he be trusted?'

Archibald looked at Samuel, who thought it may be provident not to say anything. 'I would trust him with my life or that of my lovely daughter. He is a misunderstood man of honour who brought this whole affair to my attention.'

'Then you have my thanks also. I shall recommend that you are both rewarded. Now, if you don't mind, I have matters to attend to.'

'Not at all.' Archibald put his hand in

his pocket and removed the coin that the lieutenant had paid him. He placed it on the desk in front of the captain.

'Good man.' The captain looked him straight in the eye. 'Good to know that we are both still trustworthy, my old friend.'

'Ay, it is that.' The two men nodded at each other before Samuel and Archibald left.

'To the inn?' Samuel asked.

'Oh, yes, because you have a matter of honour to fulfil.' Archibald slapped him on the back.

'I have proposed to Amelia already and I am most sincere,' Samuel began to explain.

'Good, because you are about to marry her. You have ruined her reputation and now you shall restore it. Whilst I am here I shall see her wed. Then I shall return to my beloved Prudence, inform her that the deed is done and, within the week, you shall return her to her mother. Than I have need of an oarsman for a little excursion to France, and you and I shall be busy for a month or two. Now go and bring your bride to be down. The day is young, she has a dress to find and I a priest.'

Samuel wasted no time. He leaped up the stairs two at a time and burst into her room.

Amy embraced him with such relief, she thought she would faint from it. 'You're safe! Where is Papa?' she asked nervously.

'Waiting for us downstairs,' Samuel answered almost laughing as he did so.

'What are we to do now?' Amelia asked, envisioning the long uncomfortable journey back to her mama, and the rebukes that awaited her there.

'Your father insists that I make an honourable woman of you and we are to wed, here in London, whilst he is here to give you away.'

Amelia stepped out into the city streets escorted by the two men in her life that meant everything to her and decided that, as soon as he returned home, she would thank her mama for having the foresight to seek her a suitable husband in the small harbour town of Whitby. It had been an inspired notion after all.

## The End

We do hope that you have enjoyed reading this large print book.

Did you know that all of our titles are available for purchase?

We publish a wide range of high quality large print books including:
**Romances, Mysteries, Classics**
**General Fiction**
**Non Fiction and Westerns**

Special interest titles available in large print are:
**The Little Oxford Dictionary**
**Music Book, Song Book**
**Hymn Book, Service Book**

Also available from us courtesy of Oxford University Press:
**Young Readers' Dictionary**
**(large print edition)**
**Young Readers' Thesaurus**
**(large print edition)**

For further information or a free brochure, please contact us at:
**Ulverscroft Large Print Books Ltd.,**
**The Green, Bradgate Road, Anstey,**
**Leicester, LE7 7FU, England.**
**Tel:** (00 44) **0116 236 4325**
**Fax:** (00 44) **0116 234 0205**

## THE FOOLISH HEART

## Patricia Robins

Mary Bradbourne's aunt brought her up after her parents died. When she was ten, her aunt had a son, Jackie, who was left with a mental disability as the result of an accident. Unselfish and affectionate, Mary dedicated her life to caring for him. But when she meets Dr. Paul Deal and falls in love with him she faces a dilemma. How will she be able to care for her cousin, when she knows she must follow her heart?

# HEIRS TO LOVING

## Rachel Ford

When Jenni Green went to trace her father's family in Brittany, she didn't know that she would keep running into Raoul Kerouac, known to everyone in the area as 'Monsieur Raoul'. Autocratically he organises a job for her in the local campsite, and pushes the *gendarmerie* to find Jenni's stolen handbag. Luckily they find it; unluckily Raoul sees it first — for the documents show that Jenni's real name is Eugénie Aimée Kerouac, part owner of the estate . . .

# PETTICOAT PRESS

## Sheila Lewis

It's 1901, and Eleanor Paton has ambitions to become a journalist, so she is devastated when her father appoints Stephen Walsh as the new editor to his newspaper. Stephen refuses to print her articles. Eleanor is determined to succeed, but a dangerous connection with a militant suffragette causes errors of judgement in her work. However, as her talent begins to flourish under Stephen's guidance, a family crisis threatens to part them forever — just when they have fallen in love.

# LOVE'S GAMBLE

## Louise Armstrong

When Sarah Gannon's papa gambles away the family home, she is forced to open a herbalist's shop to survive. The Duke of Whitewell, in gratitude for Sarah's visits and medicines, leaves her a generous legacy upon his death. However, the new Duke suspects the worst of their innocent relationship, and Sarah is scathing in return. With such rancour between them, she never suspects why winning back Tewit Manor hasn't made her happy. When will she realise that home is where the heart is?